TOM CLANCY'S NET FORCE

*Don't miss any of these exciting adventures
starring the teens of Net Force . . .*

VIRTUAL VANDALS

The Net Force Explorers go head-to-head with a group of teenage pranksters on-line—and find out firsthand that virtual bullets can kill you!

THE DEADLIEST GAME

The virtual Dominion of Sarxos is the most popular war game on the Net. But someone is taking the game too seriously . . .

ONE IS THE LONELIEST NUMBER

The Net Force Explorers have exiled Roddy—who sabotaged one program too many. But Roddy's created a new "playroom" to blow them away . . .

THE ULTIMATE ESCAPE

Net Force Explorer pilot Julio Cortez and his family are being held hostage. And if the proper authorities refuse to help, it'll be Net Force Explorers to the rescue!

THE GREAT RACE

A virtual space race against teams from other countries will be a blast for the Net Force Explorers. But someone will go to any extreme to sabotage the race—even murder . . .

TOM CLANCY'S
NET FORCE™

END GAME

CREATED BY

Tom Clancy and **Steve Pieczenik**

BERKLEY JAM BOOKS, NEW YORK

TOM CLANCY'S NET FORCE: END GAME

A Berkley Jam Book / published by arrangement with
Netco Partners

PRINTING HISTORY
Berkley Jam edition / October 1999

The Penguin Putnam Inc. World Wide Web site address is
http://www.penguinputnam.com

ISBN: 0-425-17113-2

BERKLEY JAM BOOKS®
Berkley Jam Books are published by The Berkley Publishing Group,
a division of Penguin Putnam Inc.,
375 Hudson Street, New York, New York 10014.
BERKLEY JAM and its logo
are trademarks belonging to Penguin Putnam Inc.

PRINTED IN THE UNITED STATES OF AMERICA

10 9 8 7 6 5 4 3 2 1

We'd like to thank the following people, without whom this book would have not been possible: Diane Duane, for help in rounding out the manuscript; Martin H. Greenberg, Larry Segriff, Denise Little, and John Helfers at Tekno Books; Mitchell Rubenstein and Laurie Silvers at BIG Entertainment; Tom Colgan of Penguin Putnam Inc.; Robert Youdelman, Esquire; Tom Mallon, Esquire; and Robert Gottlieb of the William Morris Agency, agent and friend. We much appreciated the help.

Prologue

It really was an extraordinary house. Everyone who saw the place said so. And the dark figure just outside the perimeter wall had to agree with them.

The place was quieter than usual, on this particular night. No sounds were to be heard but the offshore breeze in the palms, a dry rustling sound. The big driveway that circled around a fountain in front of the main entrance portico was empty except for a small vehicle, dark and nondescript, somebody's run-down-to-the-store car—very unlike the splendid relics of an earlier age of combustion that usually parked there on party nights. A few lights were on here and there in the front windows, one or two in some of the windows on the sides of the massive square building. But the figure out in the dark knew they were on timers. No one was home; well, almost no one . . . not that it mattered. The single occupant would never know he had been there.

He checked his watch. Two-fourteen A.M. And as he watched, a light flickered off in another of the side windows. The dark-clothed watcher nodded, for he had been expecting that. The light in question was on a timer. Over the next ten minutes, as he watched, several more of them on that side of the house went out, and then one of the lights up front, as if someone was going to bed.

No one was, of course. The single occupant of the house was already sleeping. The watcher knew which window was hers, and had noted when its light went off. He knew enough about her sleeping habits to be willing to wait awhile before moving, so for the moment he sat and appreciated the architecture.

The house had been brought over stone by stone from Venice, some ten years ago, when the area around the Campo San Maurizio had begun sinking so quickly that not even the UN Emergency Engineering Task Force, then in place in the city, could do anything about it. It was one of the first of what other countries had referred to as "temporary expatriation projects," and what the Venetians referred to bitterly as "legalized theft." Il Casa dei Malipieri had been a mostly neglected palazzo around the corner and down the canal from the church of San Maurizio. Now it was sitting resplendent in this sheltered and extremely expensive private development in the South Beach area of Miami, and it looked entirely at home—its exterior of golden limestone buffed to a rich gleam, the lemon trees from its old rear-walled garden now tastefully arranged in the middle of the acres of perfectly manicured grass in which it sat. There had been the usual problems with getting planning permission for the changes that brought the house into the twenty-first century—the interior automation, the air-conditioning, the security installations, and even the restoration of the building's stone, which had suffered badly from being progressively immersed deeper and deeper in Venice's polluted water, and exposed to the acid air and rain of an increasingly industrial part of northern Italy. The Italian authorities had insisted that the Casa dei Malipieri was just on an extended loan to its present inhabitants, and that almost nothing should be changed. The local authorities had insisted that the house was now in another country's jurisdiction, and historical questions aside, something had to be done about the sewage arrangements and other aspects of construction that would bring the house, if only temporarily, into agreement with local code. The owner of the house—that being how he thought of himself, and to hell with the comic-opera Italian government—pretty much did what he pleased with it and said loudly that that was the way it should be. Hadn't he saved the damned house, after all? Wouldn't it be at the bottom of a canal right now if he hadn't shelled out more than three million dollars to get it over here and get it in some kind of shape where human beings could live in it again?

The darkly dressed figure outside the gates, crouching down in the shelter of the shrubbery on the far side, laughed under his breath. He had heard the rich man in question do that particular riff about a hundred times now, and it got funnier every time. There was absolutely no question that Jack Ariani had done a brilliant job of restoring the house—and once the air-conditioning and the plumbing had been taken care of, he had then turned his attention to acquiring, or as he somewhat bizarrely put it, "reacquiring," every single piece of Renaissance furniture and art that could with any accuracy have been attributed to the house in its heyday when one of the great families of the city they called La Serena had lived there. Mining the Serene Empire for all the cash they could. They pumped their share into the only kind of consumption people of that place and period understood: the conspicuous kind.

The figure in the dark watched one last light go out, then softly made his way toward the little "postern" gate in the wall. They had had a pile of Titians, the Malipieri, and half a dozen other lesser-known Italian artists. They had some "early period" Michelangelos, both paintings and sculpture, piles of hardwood and gilt, fabulous tapestries and ceramics, and the best of the early Venetian glass. All kinds of precious things. That had been half a millennium ago. Half of that stuff was now in there in that house, tonight, but it was not what the dark figure had come for.

He paused by the gate, listening. No sound of car engines anywhere nearby, no footsteps, no barking dogs. There were dogs in the house sometimes, but not for purposes of guarding anything. The boss took them with him on all his business trips. There were other forms of security here . . . but the intruder knew about those, and was ready for them.

Satisfied by the depth of the quiet around him, he pulled

out the little black box he had been carrying in his pocket and touched it to the lock of the gate. The lock looked mechanical, as if it should have needed a big old key with a huge fat ward to open it, but this was an illusion—no key would have turned in that keyhole, which was full of locking equipment of an entirely different kind. The infrared variance/ induction detector in the little box sniffed around inside the lock for the chip that it knew would be there, interrogated it briefly, and sent it the command that had been the most difficult part of this whole operation to discover, since the people who had installed this locking system had gone out of business several years previously. Silently the three bolts holding the gate secure withdrew themselves. The gate, counterbalanced to open without needing to be touched, swung back.

The dark figure slipped in and touched the gate with a finger. It swung closed again. The bolts reshot themselves.

He slipped off to the right inside the wall, looking for the ancillary control box that he knew was nearby. Finding it, he touched a couple of controls on the black box he was carrying and sent the second set of signals he had prepared. Then he set off across the lawns, untroubled by any of the passive-infrared lights that would normally have come on to crisscross the path of the casual evening stroller, or the potential thief.

He bore right before reaching the driveway and its terminal circle and fountain. There was simply no way to walk quietly on gravel, and it was easier to stay on the grass, since he had no plans to try to get into the house through its front door under these circumstances. Around the side of the house he went, under three floors' worth of windows, bearing a little farther to the right to miss more gravel and the conservatory that it surrounded. Stupid idea, he thought, barbaric, pasting something like this onto the side of something that has a perfectly good open-air atrium inside. Some people have no taste.

Then he chuckled under his breath, for that was why he was here.

Out behind the conservatory there were plantings of yew and other thickly leafed ornamental trees, intended to block the view to the east, where a side street ran and some other houses could be seen. The dark figure slipped through these toward the point where they stopped, giving way to flower beds and a small herb garden, both laid out directly behind the transplanted palazzo. Here he put the small black box away, reached into his jacket, and came out with a larger one, its touch pad subdivided into many buttons.

Cautiously he stepped out onto one of the flower beds, picking a spot where he would not have to set more than one foot on a soft surface. A second step brought him out to the sandstone-slab pavement running between the flower bed and the herb garden. There he briefly stood one-footed and pulled out of another pocket a small brush, with which he brushed off the sole of the shoe that had been in the flower bed—he didn't see any reason to make life any easier for the forensics people who would be all over this area within a few hours. When the shoe was very clean, he swept the footprint he'd left behind in the garden soil out of existence, pocketed the brush again, and made for the house.

There were two sets of entrances back here: one a double pair of French doors giving onto a patio of the golden slab sandstone, another a normal door to what was now the house's downstairs utility room. The dark-dressed intruder smiled as he came to it, and paused to point the second black box at the pad by the door, touching in a string of numbers.

Nothing appeared to happen, but the shape in the darkness reached down and very softly turned the doorknob.

The door opened. He stepped inside, eased it closed again with the knob still turned, and very gently released the catch. Then he pointed the box at the security panel on the inside and touched another string of numbers into it. A light that had been green on the panel now glowed red.

He stood there in silence for a moment, then pulled down the lenses from inside the bill of the Orioles baseball cap he was wearing. Through them the world around him—washing machine, dryer, cabinets, racked and folded ironing board—had an odd, slightly underlit look, and the lighting shifted as he slowly made his way toward the door into the kitchen. He was carrying his own light source with him. The lenses were hypersensitive to infrared, and anything that was not in itself a heat source was shining slightly with reflected heat, the source of which was his own body.

The door into the kitchen stood open. He paused on the threshold, looking around. It was a large and spectacular installation, combining the best of Renaissance design with some kitchen features that had been common then, and some that would be more natural in television starships. Slick glass and matte-finished brass glittered very softly here and there in the tiny lights associated with various of the appliances. Off to one side yawned a great metal-barred rectangular space that would have been dead black in daylight, but still glowed noticeably in the dark figure's vision—the massive fifteenth-century cooking fireplace with vertical grill, its firebrick still gently exuding heat left over from an in-house barbecue held two days ago.

The dark figure made his way quietly past the center island and through to the next door, the one that led into the dining room. Here he paused for appreciation's sake as much as to listen for any sound, but the silence was total. He was alone with a huge Della Robbia dining table, sumptuously carved with swags of fruit and flowers and gleaming faintly with much gold leaf. The chairs were lined up against the walls at the moment. Overhead, a chandelier of newer Venetian glass, the kind with the colors that these days made the glass look like cheap colored plastic, hung and glowed gently in parasitic heat left over from where its lights had been turned on earlier.

Out of period, the dark figure thought critically, and passed on through into the living room. Though *room* was possibly the wrong word for an area that you would normally think of not in terms of square feet but in acres. This space took up most of the first floor of the palazzo, and was scattered with staggering amounts of furniture, not a stick of which was less than five hundred years old. He shook his head at it all. The place looked like a warehouse. The original owners would be shocked, he thought.

He turned to his left and carefully made his way toward the huge and beautiful marble stairway that curved down from the second floor, and which had probably cost more than any other part of this house to move and reassemble. Here he had to begin to watch his step—the security precautions on the stairs and much of the second floor were ones he had been unable to acquire disabling keys for. But he was not too worried about this. As in all too many domestic security installations, the people designing it had spent much too much time concentrating on heavy-duty peripheral security—as if they expected to be attacked by tanks or some wandering band of infantry—and not nearly enough on internal features. This was due to the common conception that double-level peripheral systems were likely to catch most thieves, and internal systems were not really all that necessary except as reassurance for the inhabitants.

And indeed it would have been easy enough for Jack Ariani's security installers to help him think exactly this way, with an eye to lining their own pockets . . . for exterior security was much more expensive than interior, and the IR interference-pattern lasers on the walls and the door and window security would have been much more attractive to the installers, cost-wise, than the pressure pads and interior PIRs for the inside of the house. Less trouble to maintain, too, especially with a cranky client unwilling to come to terms with the fact that half the false alarms in his last house's security installation were caused by his dogs.

So the dark figure walked quietly up the stairs, noting as he glanced at the carved banisters that Della Robbia had been here throwing fruit around again. He had no trouble at all with the pressure pads laid here and there on the treads, under the long sweep of custom-woven carpet. He had known where they all were when he came, and even if he hadn't, he could see them—the slight warmth caused by the resistance of the electricity running through them made bright patches that he could see right through the rugs. Sidestepping, or walking on the occasional rug's fringes, was all he had to do to avoid these.

And then he was out on the first landing. Here, according to his research, there was one PIR, down at the far end of the long hallway where he stood. He had no need to go higher, and he would have been unwilling to anyway, since the house sitter was sleeping up there, in the guest bedroom nearest to the master. The master was where the Titians were, and two of the Michelangelos. But the real action, from the night-walker's point of view, was down here.

Quietly he made his way down the hall, to one side of the spectacular and subtly woven floor covering that ran down it, a genuine Goebelin—*imagine putting something like that on the floor*, he thought. *Some people.* He had to step on it once or twice to avoid an occasional table, but he did so under protest.

And then he was just out of range of the PIR, and he stopped. This was the only genuinely uncertain moment of the entire operation, and he had thought for a long time about this moment before committing himself. He had disabled and reset the second-level peripherals, all the windows and doors and so forth, but he had not been able to determine absolutely whether this PIR was in the same circuit. There had been some maintenance on it lately, and his sources had not been able to tell him for sure whether this particular sensor had been tampered with or changed somehow. He would have about a quarter second to cover for himself if it hadn't.

From his other pocket, having briefly put away his main control console, he pulled out one additional control, the PIR killer. It was an unsubtle little beast, but it would do the job if it had to . . . though only for a few minutes. If the PIR came on, he would have to move much faster than he had originally planned.

Taking a deep breath, he moved forward . . . paused.

Nothing.

Another step.

Nothing.

One more . . .

He breathed out then. The PIR was dead for the moment.

All the same, his heart had begun to beat fast—and suddenly he began to feel as if it would be better if he were out of here. Just adrenaline, he thought as he took out his big control pad again and softly opened the left-hand door at the end of the hall. But even if his sudden nervousness was a side effect of blood chemistry, he was not going to ignore it.

He slipped into the room, closed the door very quietly. This was an office, or was trying to make the casual observer think it was one. In IR view very little here was warm. The registers from the central heating system glowed, along with the big computer and implant chair that had been operating late last night before Jack went away, but not much else. Any residual body heat had long since faded to the point where it was no longer visible. But the intruder knew exactly where in the room Jack had been last night, and what he had been tending to, just before he left.

Now he walked over past the big old writing desk and the hardwood filing cabinets to the wall where one of the lesser-known pictures hung, a Tintoretto that Jack was getting assayed to find out whether it was indeed a forgery. If it turned out to be real, that would be something of a joke. Jack liked it here because it was apparently a fake, a kind of symbol for other kinds of fakery in which he indulged.

The robber carefully pocketed his control pad for a moment, then lifted the Tintoretto down from the suspensor mounting and rested it against a nearby chair. He turned to look at the wall. Absolutely perfectly solid and flat, or so it seemed even to the careful glance. Looking at it with IR, though, proved otherwise. There was a broad flat shimmer of light there, a shimmer that moved and left a tweedy moiré pattern.

The dark figure pulled out the pad and tapped a long number into it, looked thoughtfully at the number, then pointed it at the wall and pressed the "activate" touch pad.

The interference pattern vanished. The dark figure let a long breath out, reached into the newly revealed cavity, and touched another long sequence of numbers into the touch pad barely visible in the darkness. There was a brief grinding noise, and then a clunk. The final door slipped open.

The intruder reached a gloved hand in and immediately found what he was looking for—the inside of the safe was extremely well insulated, since it was fireproof, and objects in it held their heat signatures for a long time. Deep in the safe, on top of some paperwork, was a little brown bag.

This was what the dark figure had come for. Not the art or the furniture or the expensive paintings and ceramics downstairs . . . nothing that traceable. Jack Ariani might like to have lots of Renaissance goodies around him, but he also liked hard currency, the harder the better, and this was about as hard as it got . . . 10.0 on the Mohs' scale. Glittering faintly, fifteen or twenty of the cut diamonds in the bag streamed into the dark figure's gloved hand. He smiled, then carefully poured them back into the little bag again; tucked them away inside his jacket, closed up the safe, and put the Tintoretto back where he had found it.

After that, it took him about as long to leave as it had taken him to come in—ten minutes, more or less. Nothing stirred in the house; not a sound was to be heard anywhere until he got outside again, closing the kitchen door behind him and using his pad to restore the alarm system to its original status. Somewhere off eastward, a dog barked as he made for the postern gate to let himself out. Twenty minutes later he was out of his blacks and into shorts and a T-shirt, riding the rapid transit line down the main street of South Beach with his gym bag over his shoulder, one more of the Saturday night crowds thronging the bars and restaurants. He hopped off the road and swung into the Shark's Tooth, where he sat down at the seafood bar and had a glass of white wine and a couple of softshell crabs. Then he went home to consider what to do about fourteen million dollars' worth of nondescript and easily disposable best blue-whites, and to plan his next job, secure in the knowledge that no one would ever, ever catch him . . . because he had the one advantage that no other burglar before him had ever had. He was his victims . . . and he was the only one who knew how to become that way.

I

It was the morning of July 31, and Megan O'Malley was sitting on one of the moons of Saturn, watching a baseball game.

Around her lay a broad cratered landscape, surprisingly bright. The brightness was due to the pale-blue methane snow that covered the surface of Rhea, all the way to the too-close horizon. Off at the very edge of things, Saturn was setting, as it did about twelve times a day, very little of it showing at the moment except the trailing edges of the rings.

Megan was sitting on the "bleachers" of what had been an old stone amphitheater in Greece. The clean design of it had impressed her, a long time ago, and she had imported it into her virtual workspace as the perfect surroundings for getting things done: functional, simple, elegant. It also had no posts to block your view, which some stadiums still did these days, even when they should have been able to work out engineering solutions that would deal with the problem. The amphitheater was perfect for baseball. Unfortunately it was unable to do anything to improve the quality of the baseball she watched in it.

Down on the "stage" the Cubs were playing Pittsburgh at Wrigley Field. It was the top of the eighth, two men out, no one on base, and currently at the plate was the only Cubs hitter who had lately shown any tendency to hit anything smaller than a barn. "Come on, Mikey," Megan muttered, "make yourself useful."

Mike Rodriguez stood there and tested his swing. On the mound, Kashiwabara wound up and let fly. Then it was strike two, and it started once again to become plain to Megan that Rodriguez was well beyond making himself useful for anything. The task was probably only possible for God, but God appeared to have left the stadium some time after the seventh-inning stretch.

The crowd, mostly local, roared good-natured scorn. Megan, sitting there on the cool stone with her legs hunched up in front of her and her arms wrapped around them, put her chin down on her knees and sighed in mild but familiar frustration. Ever since she had been old enough to pay any attention to sports, Megan had been a fan of the Cubbies. This tendency her brothers described alternatively as some bizarre sex-linked genetic problem—her grandmother was from Chicago—or as a peculiar personality trait. " 'Ever she perversely affecteth the losing side of a quarrel,' " said her older brother, quoting some obscure fantasy writer of the last century.

Megan could do little but groan at that. There was no question that the Cubbies lost. That seemed to be their purpose in life, some cranky deity having apparently designed them to remind human beings that accomplishment is fleeting and that box scores do not always reflect one's innate potential. All the same, she liked them—they just wouldn't give up—and what could she do? It was one of those early preferences that you get stuck with for life, like a duckling imprinting on a human being as its mommy, and there didn't seem anything she could do about it.

On the mound Kashiwabara looked thoughtfully at his catcher, shook his head infinitesimally, shook it again, and then nodded. The first- and third-base coaches went into a flurry of signals that made them look like Reform Catholics with sudden cases of Saint Vitus's dance.

"Megs?" came the voice of one of her brothers out of the air. "You still in there abusing yourself?"

Megan rolled her eyes. "If by that you mean am I looking at last night's game," she said, "yes."

"Gonna stunt your growth that way."

She grimaced. "Was there a reason for this call," she said, "or were you just trying to be pointlessly annoying? And not doing too well at it, I might add."

"I have two words for you," Seán said. "Fourteen-nothing, Pirates."

"Three words, O innumerate one," Megan said.

"And Dad just called. He'll be home in fifteen minutes."

"Hey, great! I'll be right out." She jumped up.

As she did, Kashiwabara leaned back and let loose a pitch that appeared to have its own independent guidance system. It looked like a big fat one, and Mikey locked onto it and swung—just as the pitch abruptly dropped about twelve inches in the air, straight down, and completely out of the area Rodriguez was hitting into. "How does he do that?" Megan muttered as Mikey stared at where the ball had been, and where it wasn't now. Then he chucked his bat dejectedly off to one side and started for the dugout to get his glove as the Pirates outfield came jogging in.

Megan sighed and walked down the steps of the amphitheater toward the bottom level, the staging area where she did her computer work and watched games like this. She paused there a moment, annoyed, and then walked straight through the interface onto the "field," strolled up next to Rodriguez as he made his way toward the dugout, and put her fist forcefully right through his head.

Being only a processed image from the holocast last night, he didn't notice. "Wouldn't I just love to do that to you in person, you waste of time," Megan muttered, "except that it would upset your kids. They should file you under AAA and ship you off to Iowa."

He just walked away, sad looking, as he had last night. Megan sighed and walked away again as the Cubs outfield headed off past her. "All right," she said to the computer, "save it for later."

"Saved," said the pleasant female voice her computer used. The field vanished, replaced by the white marble floor of her amphitheater's stage, the chair she usually sat in while working in here, and many small rotating colored or glowing cubes, spheres, and pyramids, the visual "thumbnail" indicators for various files and messages awaiting her attention. "Handle mail now?"

Megan looked at it all and shook her head. *Where does all this come from?* Every morning her box was full of ads, cyberspam, virtual "flyers" for local restaurants and magazine subscriptions, get-rich-quick schemes, chain letters, and junk mail . . . and no matter how she tweaked her mail filters, it just seemed to keep getting worse. She understood that the Net had always been something of an anarchy zone since its inception, but it seemed to be getting more and more that way over time. *We're rapidly approaching the time when we'll achieve peace on Earth, because everyone will be spending all their time cleaning out their mailboxes. . . .*

She smiled slightly as she walked among the various rotating solids, peering at them to see if any of them had message tags on them that made them look even vaguely important. Some of them had to do with class assignments for her senior year, but she didn't need to look at those yet, and she was determined not to at least until the middle of August. School would start soon enough, and there was no need to think about it just now. Meanwhile, none of the rest of the messages were of any concern to her at all. "Naah," she said. "Save it all for later on."

"Break interface now?"

"Yes, please."

There came the usual faint physical sensation like having to sneeze and not being able to. Then Megan found herself once again looking across the room at the general purpose/net access computer in her dad and mom's den.

She got up out of the lineup chair, stretching, and smiling slightly at the way the front of the computer's implant-access port was for once not blocked by a half-toppling pile of books. And the desks were clean, too. Her mom always tidied up after herself after she had been working, claiming that order was the heart of a journalist's art. But her dad insisted that it was a constitutional right for a writer to be messy.

When he was working, every available horizontal surface became covered with open books, closed books, books on top of each other holding each other open, and they stayed that way until he had finished tracking down whatever abstruse piece of information he was hunting for that particular novel or whatever. The curtains were open, now, the blinds were up, and the desks were clean. They had been that way for nearly a week, since Megan's dad had gone off on his latest lecture gig, to Xanadu of all places. But shortly after the couple of hours it took her dad to get settled in again, the desks would be invisible, the blinds would be down and the curtains would be shut, making a cave of the den again, one suitable for its shuffling, growling inhabitant, a writer hunting down his prey.

Megan stretched one more time and ambled out of the den down the hall and into the kitchen. She would be glad to have her dad back. She missed him, especially this time of year when the older brothers were back from college. It could be fun having all her siblings around, but he was a stabilizing influence on them—meaning he was sometimes able to keep them from eating everything in the house in a matter of a day or so. Collectively they had a talent for stripping a kitchen bare that army ants would have envied.

And sure enough, as Megan came into the bright sunny kitchen, there were Sean and Paul, with their heads stuck in the refrigerator. Sean was already gnawing on a chicken leg. Paul was groping around in the salad drawer, while holding half a head of lettuce in his free hand. Rory was sitting at the kitchen table putting away oatmeal with a side of bacon like there was no tomorrow.

"Lettuce for breakfast?" Megan said. "Paul, are you worrying about your weight again? You're nuts."

"I wouldn't get too judgmental about other people's sanity if I were you," Sean said, not coming out of the fridge. "Fourteen nothing!"

"Could have been worse, the way the Cubs were playing," Rory said, gulping down some coffee.

"Please," Megan said, and went to make herself some tea. "Not until I get some caffeine in me."

She went over to the stove for the kettle, filled it at the sink, and put it on to boil, then wandered over to the counter where the tea- and coffee-making things lived, fished out two Lapsang souchong teabags, and put one in a mug from the mug tree. A vague rustling sound was followed by her oldest brother, Mike, heading through the kitchen and making for the back door while struggling his way into a bright orange whole-body kayaking coverall. The effect, with all the Day-Glo stripes and hazard flashes, was very striking, but Megan still thought it made him look like a toddler in a snowsuit, and it went *ziffziffziff* in exactly the same way every time he took a step.

"Morning, Mike," Megan said.

"Nnnggghhh," Mike said, and let the kitchen door slam behind him as someone out in front of the house started honking the horn.

"Must have been a tough night last night," Sean commented from inside the refrigerator.

"As if you ever stopped eating long enough to notice," Megan said, reaching in past him for the milk. The kettle began to whistle. She turned to get it, and Sean grinned at her and made what would have normally been a pretty effective aikido move—one of the foot sweeps—except that Megan's body reacted to it before her brain did, and all of a sudden he was sitting on the floor with half a roast chicken in his lap.

"Nice catch," Megan said mildly, and stepped over him to take the kettle off the stove. "Better get that back in the fridge before Dad turns up and sees you."

She poured boiling water into her mug and was careful not to let them see her smile. Megan had started martial arts training at almost the same time the older brothers had, but much younger than they had, with the usual result. She was better at it than they were . . . though she went to some trouble not to rub their noses in the fact. Unless they forced her to, which was another matter entirely.

A high whine from outside was a cab, settling into the driveway their house shared with the one next door. Megan's brothers went into high-speed clean-up-the-wreckage mode. Megan went looking for the sugar bowl.

A door slammed outside, and the whine receded. A moment later the back door opened, and her dad was standing there, shedding suitcases and briefcases and shopping bags and other paraphernalia of travel. Looking at him, you could see from which side her brothers had acquired the family gene for tallness. He was balding a little on top, still lean in his early fifties, and very casually and comfortably dressed. Her brothers went to hug him briefly. "Hey, you guys," Megan's dad said, "what about it? You behave yourselves?"

"Yeah," and "Of course," they said. Megan did not laugh, out loud anyway. Her dad gave her a smile. "Is your mom up?"

"Not yet," Paul said before Megan could open her mouth. "She had a late deadline last night, something for *Time-Online*. Said she was going to sleep in."

"Sensible woman," said Megan's dad, dropping himself into one of the kitchen chairs and yawning. "Don't know what possessed me to let the travel agent talk me into the eight o'clock flight. Two hours of check-in, then endless standing around . . . Never again just yet."

Megan gave him her tea and went to make herself another cup as her brothers went off about their own business. "You didn't ask me what I brought you," her dad said.

Megan gave him a droll look. That had been a standing joke between them since she'd been about twelve, the time she noticed that her brothers' demands in this regard were getting on her father's nerves. "Later," she said now, as she had when she was twelve. "So how was Xanadu?"

"Well, a little stirred up," her dad said, drinking the tea.

"Don't tell me you started another riot."

He looked slightly rueful. He had spoken at a civil-liberties seminar a couple of months before, with very unexpected results. "Not this time. No, the trouble was someone else's. Seems one of their clients' houses was broken into. Someone stole valuables to the tune of twenty million dollars or so. . . ."

Megan sat down with her own tea across the table from

her father. "Who has twenty million dollars' worth of stuff in their house? But I didn't hear anything on the news."

"Well." He looked a little amused. "No, you wouldn't have. I happened to be in the Xanadu corporate offices the morning before last, and I heard a little something I shouldn't have."

Megan raised her eyebrows at that, but said nothing. Over the past ten years she had started to notice that, for a mystery writer and general freelancer, her father seemed to know a lot of important people—more important people than mystery writers normally knew anyway. He kept claiming that he met them "while doing research," but Megan was not so gullible as to completely believe him anymore. Besides, he knew James Winters at Net Force . . . and that by itself suggested a certain access to inside information, as Megan had discovered since joining the Net Force Explorers and meeting Winters herself.

"Look," Megan said, "could you start at the beginning? Was it incredibly luxurious and decadent, the resort? Were there hundreds of billionaires there?"

Her father made a resigned face. "At least tens. Yes, it was pretty posh . . . and the food was good, too." He had another drink of the tea. "Honey, it's very much like a terrific six-star hotel, as far as the buildings go . . . and they go on for miles. Beautiful antique furnishings, three staff to every guest, hot and cold running everything. Massive grounds, championship golf course, sauna park, double Olympic pools, riding, snorkeling, scuba, private beach . . ." He yawned. "All very sybaritic. I missed your mother. I wish she could have cleared her schedule, but . . ."

"But did you try out the virtual stuff?" she nearly shrieked, for this was the part that had made Megan nearly wild with excitement when the word came through that her father had been asked to lecture there. It was an incredible opportunity. Xanadu was famous everywhere, not just for the luxurious, exclusive private island and all the rest of it, but for the exotic and elaborate virtual "pavilions" it built for its millionaire clients. Xanadu's founder had been a gifted programmer with the financial backing and expertise to turn his particular gift into something more valuable than gold. In this case, the something was a proprietary system that produced custom-tailored virtual experience of such stunning inventiveness and deep emotional involvement that nothing else available in this world, real or virtual, matched it. And it was all yours . . . at a hefty price . . . for the duration of the time you bought in the system.

Time in the Xanadu virtual pavilions did not come cheap, and it became even more expensive when you considered that those virtual experiences were not transmitted along the Net, as almost everything else was these days, but had to be experienced directly at the Xanadu resort site, east of the Bahamas. The Xanadu people claimed that their proprietary software ran at too high a bandwidth for the public Net system to successfully transmit it. Having heard this, Megan didn't buy it for a minute—the Net's bandwidth doubled, it seemed, every couple of months, and home hardware's ability to keep up with it increased routinely as well. But refusing to let proprietary software and routines be transmitted out of Xanadu's system struck her as a smart way to keep them secure. What was routinely available in the world would get hacked soon enough . . . and Xanadu's inventor stood to lose billions in potential licensing and the income of future years if it did.

"How can you make that kind of noise this time of the morning?" her father said, rubbing his forehead. "Please— yes, I tried one of the 'open' pavilions." He stretched his legs out and leaned back in his chair. "Nothing kinky," he added, noticing the look she gave him.

"What a shame," Megan said, with a very small smile.

"That's enough out of you, young lady." He gave her the same smile back, but with a slight edge on it. "I know they're famous for their 'fantasy,' but that doesn't particularly interest me. The one I looked into was 'Escape from Pompeii.' Gruesome."

"How was the volcano?"

"Cataclysmic," her father said. "The earth moved. Ashes rained from the sky. It's not like you don't know how that story ends, Megan."

She grinned. "Yeah, but it's the fullness of the experience, isn't that what their ads say? 'Even better than the real thing.' ''

"Well, it was pretty intense," her father said, and rubbed his scalp absently. "It was even worse than that time in Sicily. I'm just glad the burns weren't real, though I would have sworn they were at the time."

"Wow," Megan said. "So who were the people you were teaching? Anybody famous?"

"Some of them," her father said. "Not that that made them particularly interesting. Some of them just came to the workshops I was running because it was something to do after breakfast." His expression became tinged with annoyance. "The few who were genuinely interested in writing either didn't need to do anything like that for a living, because they were already rolling in more money than I've ever seen, or else they were completely unteachable." He sighed.

"I thought you said no one was unteachable."

"These particular people," her father said reluctantly, "made me reassess my theory. They didn't think what I was doing was any kind of teaching. They thought I was entertainment. Or if they didn't, there were those whose egos suggested that it was impossible for any mere mortal to teach them anything they didn't know already. Money, I understand, can do that to you."

Her dad drank more tea, then laughed a little. "I don't know, honey. They certainly paid me well enough, and the surroundings were gorgeous . . . no question, it's the kind of place I'd like to take your mom for a vacation."

"Away from us."

"Did I say that?" He gave her an amused look. "If I could afford it, anyway, which I can't any time soon. But the virtual side of the place is such a draw that I don't know why they bother asking people to come in and do the cruise-circuit kind of thing . . . lectures on writing, and cooking demonstrations, and aerobics classes. Most people, even billionaires, having paid that kind of money to go to Xanadu, are intent on getting their money's worth . . . and they don't care much about the sideshows in the circus. Certainly not the kind of dog and pony show I run."

Megan frowned at him. "Stop that! You're a good teacher! And you write pretty good stuff. For a dad."

He fumbled one-handed around the cluttered table for a notepad. "I want that in writing," he said, "pardon the pun. Anyway, I don't think I'll bother doing it again."

Megan gave him a curious look. "You mean they asked you to?"

"Not right then. They suggested they might. But, Megan, I don't know. All that rich food . . ."

"All that lobster and caviar!" she cried. "All that decadence!"

"Decadence is overrated," her father said, "and usually has too much cholesterol." He yawned again.

"It's just your blood sugar saying that," Megan said. "So what about this guy and the twenty million dollars?"

"Oh. He was one of the new intake of guests—they overlap small groups, so as not to overload the place's facilities, apparently."

Or to control how many people have access to the software at any one time, Megan thought.

"He can't have been there more than a day or two. Some kind of property speculator based in Miami. He was about to take delivery on some sort of spectacular Renaissance Italian scenario." Her father gave Megan another of those wry looks. "In fact, he didn't stop talking about it from the moment he arrived. He could have been on the U.S. Olympic Boring team. Endless blather about this historic moment he was going to re-create—what was it—oh, yes. Some sword fight in the middle of Venice in 1532. Or was it Milan? Don't ask me for details. After the first six repetitions or so I just tried to avoid him. Anyway, while he was boring us, somebody got into his house in Miami—no one's sure how. Apparently he'd spent a fortune having the place wired up like a fortress. Not that it mattered, because the thief, or thieves, got away with a pile of diamonds he kept somewhere in there, in a safe." Her father shook his head. "I swear, why don't people put things like that in banks? He might as well just have stuffed them in a mattress. Once word gets out that you have something that valuable in your house, if someone wants it, they're going to get it."

"What did he do?"

"Swore a blue streak and called his private hopper," said her father, finishing the tea, "and was gone about ten minutes after the news came through. Breakfast time, it was." Her father smiled slightly. "How peaceful breakfast was without him. I was able to settle in and really enjoy my kipper."

Megan made a face. Smoked fish was not high on her list of things to eat at breakfast. "You're weird. Was that what you heard them talking about in the office?"

"Boy, you're a nosy bird this morning," her father said. "Well, that, yes, but apparently they were concerned about more than just the scandal of it all. It seems like whoever engineered the break-in had access to at least some of Mr. Ariani's—that was his name, Jack Ariani—some of his Net ID. Passwords, encryption schemes, things like that: virtual-access ID, the kind of stuff that should have been most secure. No one was being very forthcoming about the details. But apparently they were getting ready to call Net Force in."

Megan's eyes went wide, both at that news, and at the realization that her father had been withholding this particular piece of information until the very end. "You mean," she said, "that the people at Xanadu think someone working for them might have been involved? That someone 'inside' was . . . I don't know, stealing personal virtual-access data and selling it?"

"They weren't saying a lot about their own suspicions when I was in there," her father said. "But it doesn't take much to work it out for yourself. I would imagine the Xanadu people are starting to worry that if something isn't done, they're mostly going to be famous for being sabotaged."

Megan sat back in her chair, looking up as Paul headed out through the kitchen in something of a rush. "Later, Dad, Megs," he said, and was gone before either of them had a chance to say a word. The back door slammed.

"Where's he off to? Oh, never mind, it's soccer on Thursdays, isn't it?" Her dad rubbed the top of his head again.

"Dad," she said, "are you sure you don't want to go back there?"

He looked at her, a little bemused. "Hey, I just got home. You want to get rid of me already?"

"No," Megan said, "of course not . . ." But something had occurred to her, and she wanted to get back into the Net as soon as she could. "You're looking awful tired," she said. "You should go in and take a nap."

"And wake your mom up before she's ready? You *do* want to get rid of me."

Now Sean plunged through the kitchen on his way out. "Later," he said to the two at the table, and was gone a moment later.

"Football," said Megan.

"I can't cope with even the thought of it," her father said, and got up slowly. "I think I'll go take my chances with your mother. I brought her back that butter amber necklace she saw in the Met catalog, anyway. Maybe she'll let me live."

Megan grinned at her father as he ambled off down the hall. She waited until she heard the master bedroom door close, then made her way back down to the den, to get on the Net again.

Normally she would have been rather shy about the idea of calling James Winters first. As titular head of the Net Force Explorers, he was someone she did not want to annoy. It was her intention to work for the organization some day, if she had anything to say about it. There was no career that struck her as more interesting, nothing more cutting edge than this—the investigation and policing of the virtual frontier, constantly being opened up, explored, exploited, and abused by all kinds of people. It needed sharp people to police it, and Megan intended to be one of them. She knew, though, that the decision as to whether she would eventually become an adult operative of Net Force, after this early flirtation, would be made mostly by James Winters. She knew better than to make a nuisance of herself to someone who could determine whether or not she would be allowed into the career that she wanted more than anything else in the world—into the majors, as it were, after this early work in the triple-A leagues.

At the same time she refused to be a coward about it. When dealing with the Net, or any other important part of life, hesitation was not something that would get you very far, especially when a hunch or an idea bit you hard enough . . . and this one had bitten Megan fairly hard, for reasons she didn't fully understand. She didn't think they had all that much to do with the attractions of a six-star millionaires' resort. She hoped they didn't.

All the same, she swallowed, feeling a bit dry-mouthed as she sat down in the big chair in front of the computer, lined up the access implant tucked under the thin skin at the side of her neck, and closed her eyes, doing the small mental "movement" that activated her Net access. A feeling like an aborted sneeze—

She was standing at the top of her amphitheater again, looking down at the staging area, now bare and white. Above it, away across the methane snow, Saturn hung fat and golden in a black sky blazing with stars. She walked down the stairs to where her own work chair sat—a rather more plump and cushy version of the implant chair.

Hovering in the air on all sides were all those cubes and spheres and pyramids of E-mail. "Ready?" Megan said to the computer, sitting down.

"Ready."

"Make me a box and put all the waiting mail in it," Megan said. "I'll take care of it later."

A small neat crate appeared off to one side, and the "thumbnail" solids obediently floated off and stacked themselves in it, like so many children's blocks.

"All right," Megan said. "Live chat mode."

"Address?"

"James Winters."

"Priority?"

"Normal." If he was busy, his system would refuse a normal-priority call without bothering him.

She sat and waited while the request routed itself through the system. It always felt a little like sneezing—nothing seemed different, then—boom—there she was.

Her surroundings flickered, and suddenly she was sitting in her chair, not on her staging area, but inside the door of James Winters's office. It looked fairly ordinary in a governmental way—plain pale-green walls ornamented only with a couple of liquid-crystal message boards covered with notes and personnel information, the usual metal and composite desk, well covered with paperwork and charts and disks and data storage solids, many with sticky notes or note crystals adhering to them, and behind the desk the man himself—tall, lean, a strongly carved face with startling blue-gray eyes looking up from his paperwork at Megan with an expression of mild interest. His Marine buzz-cut looked shorter than usual. Probably the haircut was new.

"Megan," he said. "Good morning. Why aren't you out in this beautiful sunshine?" He looked somewhat regretfully at the window. "I wish I were."

She smiled slightly. Megan knew from scuttlebutt among the various Net Force Explorers that Winters's vacation had been rescheduled for what was apparently the third time this year. No one was clear, though, whether this was something that had been done to him from above, or whether Winters's concern for the ongoing business of his office had made him reschedule his vacation himself. He was well known not to enjoy leaving his office when anything important was going on . . . and James Winters thought that just about anything to do with Net Force was important.

"I've had enough sunshine for the moment," Megan said. "My brothers can spend every day out in it kicking footballs and soccer balls around if they want to. I'm enjoying the shade."

"So it seems." He glanced "past" her at Megan's workspace. "Snow . . . I wouldn't mind getting away for some skiing."

"You wouldn't like it here," Megan said, looking briefly over her shoulder. "If you pick up too much speed on it, the methane snow sublimates right out from under you with the heat of the friction. I tried some glacier skiing here once." She gave him a rueful look. "It didn't work too well. The crevasses here are half a mile deep."

"Ouch," Winters said. "I'll take a rain check. Though I doubt it rains much there, either. So what can I do for you this morning?"

"Well, I have a couple of questions for you," Megan said. "You probably know, my dad just got back from Xanadu—"

She wasn't absolutely sure that he knew, but with Winters it was usually wiser to assume that he did. He tended to follow the family lives of his Net Force Explorers fairly closely, a tendency founded as much in genuine affection for them as in concern for their safety.

"I heard something about that," he said. "How did he like it?"

"Mixed," Megan said. "I don't think the student body was everything he would have liked it to be. Otherwise, he had fun there. But he told me that one of the clients had just been robbed."

"Mmm-hmm," Winters said, completely noncommittally, putting down the pen he had been holding. He leaned his elbows on the desk, laced his fingers together, and put his chin down on them for a moment.

Megan swallowed. The man could make himself unreadable at a moment's notice. It was very unnerving. "He mentioned," Megan said, "that this was not the first attack on their clients that the Xanadu people had had. And that the evidence so far seemed to point to someone getting hold of virtual-access information from clients—electronic signatures, things like that—and using them out in the real world, or other parts of the virtual world, to commit crimes."

"Your dad said that to you, did he?" Winters said.

Megan gulped again. "Not that precisely," she said. "Some of this is my inference from what Dad said he overheard in the Xanadu offices."

Winters looked at her for a moment, then nodded. "All right. Always be careful with your attributions, Megan. They can come back and haunt you later. Go on."

"Well," she said after a moment collecting her thoughts, "this sounds really nasty. If someone there is selling people's virtual IDs, then you have two separate problems. First of all, all Net-access IDs of the really important kinds are supposed to be unforgeable. After all, they're based on physical ID like DNA matching and close iridology scans, or the new high-accuracy fingerprint scanning.

"But the second problem is worse." Megan looked out Winters's window at a small brown bird that was suddenly clinging to the windowsill, pecking at the glass. "If Net access information like this, forged or unforged—information that's supposed to be safely encrypted and locked to one personality—is being passed around . . . then it lends itself to impersonation. People pretending that they're other people . . . that they're supposed to be in that bank account, for example, or that virtual business meeting. It's easy to alter appearances in the Net. Lots of people do it for their own security. But if you can fake the ID underlying it as well . . ."

She trailed off. Winters was holding quite still. Behind him, at the window, the tapping went on.

"That's a very good summation," he said. "It fairly closely mirrors a conversation I had the other day with the people at Xanadu."

She breathed out. So far, so good.

He leaned back and looked at her for a moment more. "All right," he said. "Let me share a little background with you. This was not the first incident of this kind, but certainly it was the most blatant. There have been some minor security slippages among recent visitors to Xanadu. Nothing all that major, at first. People's Net access computers or systems have been compromised, data looked at, sometimes erased, sometimes stolen . . . we think. Those first few offenses weren't considered by the Xanadu people to be connected, first of all for lack of data, and secondly because they seemed to be, well, rather petty." Winters shrugged. "In one case, someone's address book was erased. In another, one directory of a lady's saved E-mail was deleted. Nothing that she thought was all that important. Xanadu thought that the fact that their clients were involved was probably coincidental. They thought some kind of ordinary hacker was responsible."

Winters pushed his chair back a little farther. "Then the break-ins began to get more serious. One client's bank records were destroyed. Another client had someone interfere, virtually, in a negotiation they were conducting. Someone masquerading as the Xanadu client sent various participants in that negotiation messages that conflicted with one another. The deal fell apart. Hundreds of thousands of dollars down the drain, apparently.''

Megan blinked at that. "Then this last event occurred," Winters said. "The Jack Ariani business. You'll notice that I'm not shy about mentioning his name. Well, old Jack brought this on himself, I'm afraid. He has a couple of RICO investigations working on him. I don't know if the FBI are going to be able to make them stick. Jack has been a very slick operator, and he's been expert at covering his tracks. But this time he may have been a little too slick for himself. Word got out about the diamonds he was keeping in his place, and someone went to some trouble to steal enough of his Net-access ID and other personal security information to be able to walk right into his house and out again with the diamonds. Now, Jack hadn't insured the stones yet, because of course the insurance company wanted information about the provenance of the diamonds . . . and Jack had only just had time to fake up the papers. He almost certainly extorted the diamonds from the head of a big Colombian crime syndicate. We can't prove that, of course. Jack's so resourceful that even the IRS hasn't been able to pin anything on him. But it seems Mr. Jack Ariani finally made a few mistakes. I wouldn't want to be the thief when Jack finds him.''

Winters smiled slightly. "So this last crime is amusing, maybe, considering how many people we think Jack has subjected to similar stings in the past, but it's still a crime, and it suggests much worse to come. Someone expert in the expropriation and use of this kind of security data could wreak all kinds of havoc. And, additionally, the people who visit Xanadu are not your ordinary people. They are the captains of industry, the seriously famous, and the seriously rich. Some of them are highly connected to various governments around the world. Some of them routinely handle very classified material indeed. If word gets out about this, Xanadu's business could crash, which would have a number of unpleasant results. At the same time, if word doesn't get out, and someone important enough goes there and has their security compromised . . . the number of unpleasant results could get completely out of hand. It could start a war somewhere.''

He folded his arms on his desk again. ''So,'' Winters said, ''the sooner this gets handled, the better.''

''So you're going to be sending Net Force operatives in there,'' said Megan.

''Certainly,'' Winters said, ''that would seem like a sensible thing to do.''

He didn't say anything further. Megan squirmed a little but tried not to let it show. ''Mr. Winters,'' she said, ''could I suggest something else that seems sensible? To me, anyway.''

He nodded.

Megan swallowed.

''It's going to be a little hard to establish credible covers for Net Force ops at short notice that aren't still going to make them stick out in Xanadu like sore thumbs,'' Megan said. ''Especially since, if there is someone working 'inside' there, they're likely to find out about it in a hurry. What about putting in someone who wouldn't stick out so much? Somebody that the bad guys wouldn't notice. Like maybe a kid.''

He just looked at her.

I won't squirm anymore, I will not. The worst he can do is tell me to—

''You mean . . . like you,'' Winters said. His expression was just slightly amused.

''It's not like I wouldn't have an excuse,'' Megan said, ''assuming Dad can get them to approve. He was saying he thought they might ask him back. What could be more natural for him to do than to take his daughter along? He would have taken Mom last time—the arrangement was for two—but she couldn't make it. That *TimeOnline* thing. Those people are slave drivers.''

Winters grinned at her then. ''You sound like Mark Gridley. He's always telling his folks that they work too hard. Well,'' he said after a moment. ''Analysis and synthesis have always been your strong suit, haven't they? Plus you have any analyst's most important characteristic: you're incurably nosy.''

Megan flushed hot and desperately hoped that she wasn't blushing as ferociously as she felt she was.

''I don't know,'' Winters said, and looked out the window. ''There are a lot of things that could go wrong here. And the main problem is the computer situation . . . which, forgive me, isn't really your specialty.''

''But the issue isn't so much what's being done with the computers there,'' Megan said. ''If that was all it was about, I'd say, sure, send Mark Gridley or somebody who can make machines sing and dance. But the question here is who's doing it. I'm as likely to get a lead on that as anyone else. Maybe more likely.''

Then she sat very still as Winters frowned, and Megan was suddenly afraid she had said too much. *Shut up, shut up,* the inside of her mind was yelling at her, *you've blown it!*

Winters looked thoughtfully at her for a few moments. Then he said, ''Have you discussed this idea with your father?''

''Not yet,'' she said. Then Megan added, ''I think he may suspect that something like this is on my mind. But when he does, he usually doesn't mention anything until I bring the subject up myself.''

Winters's eyebrows shot up. ''Your father,'' he said, ''is a wise man, but I've had opportunity to notice that before.'' Megan was burning to ask him exactly how and why—the connection between Winters and her father was rather obscure to her—but she knew better than to do it right now.

Captain Winters sighed. ''Megan,'' he said, ''it was very proactive of you to bring this to me. All I can do at the moment is take it under advisement. And I think I know the perfect way to do what you're asking. But we have to look into things at our end first, and it may take a little while. Also, I wouldn't be the only one who would have to sign off on this particular idea. There are safety issues, too, to consider if we involve you or someone like you. And there are other people who would have to be convinced. The minute I have any hard news for you, I'll pass it on.''

Megan's heart sank. She had been hoping for a clear "yes" or "no" on the spot. Then she was distracted by something tapping at the window again. Winters turned to look at it. "Oh," he said, "it's LBJ."

Huh? Megan thought. The small brown bird was there again, hammering at the window as if it wanted to come in, but it looked nothing like the president from the previous century. "Sorry?"

"LBJ," Winters said. " 'Little Brown Job.' It's a birders' term. I run that "window" as a virtual mirror of the situation outside my dining room window at home. I put a feeder out for the birds in the wintertime. Some of them are of the opinion that winter doesn't come soon enough." He sighed again. "I'm beginning to feel that way myself. I don't think I'm ever going to get away for some skiing . . . even on methane." He glanced briefly down at the piled-up work on his desk, then up again. "Was there anything else?"

"No," Megan said, "that was it."

Winters nodded. "I'll be in touch, then. And, Megan . . . thanks. I appreciate your commitment. We'll see what happens."

Winters and his office flickered out, and Megan found herself looking at Saturn again, setting now, a fat crescent behind sharp shadowed rings like sickles.

Phooey, she thought, and got up, heading up the stairs of her amphitheater. She supposed she couldn't blame Winters for his caution. But at the same time, she thought, *if they don't do something pretty quick, there's going to be big trouble*.

Now, though, she thought as she broke the connection to her workspace and found herself sitting in the den again, *I get to deal with the hardest part of being a Net Force Explorer.*

The waiting . . .

2

In a large and handsome office building in London, not too far from the Palace of Westminster, Harold Winston-Thomas sat and made a few last notes on the electronic scribble pad in his lap. The beautiful old teak-paneled office around him was on a corner of the building in Old Church Street, third floor up, with a spectacular view of the river. He had waited nearly twenty years for it, until one of the youngest of the senior partners had the grace to die suddenly while up in Scotland, golfing at the Royal and Ancient. Since then he had taken great care to do nothing that would imperil his own hold on that office, finally granted to him after a long period of "deliberation among the other senior partners," which he suspected had mostly been intended to make him suffer. It had been an initiation, a cruel one, as nasty as any schoolboy midnight ritual of initiation into some secret club.

He had taken it without so much as a whimper, though, and finally they had given up and voted him the package for which he had waited so long—the office, the stock options, the membership in the club, and the caseload that would make a millionaire of him, as it had made all of them in the fullness of time.

Harold leaned back and looked at the pad one last time. A barrister with Tollsworth, Barrington-Smythe, and Hobart could expect to have the best cases, from the best class of society, dropped into his lap over time, mostly because of the founder's relations. The founder, Mr. Tollsworth, had been first a lowly solicitor, then eventually a barrister, and much later had been called within the bar to accept the title of K.C., King's Counselor, so that he could plead before the High Court. But much more important than that, much more important than Tollsworth's legal acumen (which was moderate) and his skill in research (which was admittedly better than average) were his connections, by marriage, to two separate baronetcies and to the Duchy of Lancaster, which owned about half the best real estate in London. People had assumed, correctly, that someone now part of the family into which Tollsworth had married would understand the needs and concerns of old money—to keep itself private, to keep it growing, to keep it out of others' hands whenever possible. Such people came to him when involved in lawsuits that threatened to lose them control of that money to lesser powers—business types, nouveaux riches, the Inland Revenue—and Tollsworth always knew how to win. Whatever his other qualifications, he simply had the gift for coming out on top.

He passed that reputation to his partners and their successors. As a result, they, too, usually came out on top. Self-fulfilling prophecy operates as routinely and blindly in the legal profession as elsewhere. Harold, himself, knew how to milk that reputation for all it was worth. He would be doing so this afternoon. He sat back, looking at the pad, and started doing simple sums in his head as to the kind of charges he would be able to make for the next six months' work on this particular case. All the sums had a most satisfactory number of zeroes after them. *Time to start checking the estate agents' ads in* The Field *again,* he thought. *Marcia has been complaining that she needs more bedrooms. At least twenty. Something nice in the Cotswolds . . .*

A soft knock sounded on the other side of the door. "Come," he said.

After a moment his secretary put her head in. "Mr. St. Regis will be on the secure link in five minutes, sir," she said.

"Very good, Carol," Harold said, and got up. "I won't be more than twenty minutes or so. Please call the Members' Tea Room and tell George to expect me for half twelve."

"Yes, sir."

She swung the door open for him to pass her. Harold went down the thick-carpeted hall, past the bookshelves made to fit the hundreds of volumes of case studies, past the doors to other partners' offices, eyeing them as he went. Some of them were more choice than his. Well, time enough to think about that later. His present one served his needs well enough, in terms of space as well as of status, and they couldn't all live forever. Whereas he was young and fit, and took good care of himself. *Some day,* he thought, *all this will be mine. . . .*

The virtual reality equipment was beautifully concealed inside of what seemed to be a seventeenth-century boardroom, and the workspace programmed into the room's computer exactly duplicated the room's splendid marquetry, apparently shipped here wholesale from France by Charles II for one of his mistresses. The appropriateness of that provenance made Harold smile slightly now as he closed the door and secured it, by this action soundproofing the room and activating the system logs.

He sat down in the huge leather chair, made himself comfortable, positioned his pad, with its own link to the computer, where he could see it, and then aligned his implant with the master access console, tastefully hidden inside a polished Louis XIII ebony breakfront.

He felt the usual slight shudder, and the room wavered and settled down again. It appeared exactly as it had before, but what Harold now saw was the room's double in Netspace, its virtual twin. That door opened, and his client came in.

Harold rose to meet him. It was a standard enough courtesy, though in Harold's case he hardly meant it. His client had gotten himself into an extremely foolish position, one where the newspapers felt they could safely attack him. He had become a perfect example of the phrase "more money than sense." Apparently the best education that money could buy in this country still could not make a man wise. Handsome the client was, but that had gotten him into this mess, and presently counted for little. He sat his tall, rangy frame down in the chair on the opposite side of the boardroom table, shot his cuffs from under the sleeves of the five-thousand-pound suit, and said, "Thanks for taking the time to see me, Harold."

"Always a pleasure," Harold said, and this was true insofar as it meant a chance to bill for another hour at the usual rates. "I take it this has to do with something not already on our schedule for this week."

"Yes," the man said, and sat back in the chair, running his hands through his sandy hair in a gesture of embarrassment. "Look . . . it's this way. I've been thinking about it, and I've decided . . . I'm going to drop the court action."

"What?" Harold said, sitting bolt upright in the chair. "I mean . . . sorry?"

"I'm going to drop it."

"But . . ." Harold had to stop and take a breath to calm himself. "Richard, it's taken three years for us to get this far. The paper has made you spend a great deal of money, tried desperately to tire you out. It's hardly a month since we got leave to appeal the lower court's decision. With the new evidence that's come out about how they've set you up, the pictures, that third woman . . . you've got them right where you want them at last. Another few months and it'll be all over . . . and your good reputation will be restored." *Not to mention that the court is likely to award you costs, and substantial damages. Award* us *costs and substantial damages . . .*

"I know," Richard said, looking very uncomfortable. "Harold, I just can't take it anymore. The stress has started to become too much. I've been having physical problems . . . chest pains. My doctor tells me that the stress has to stop, before it turns into something worse, something a lot more sudden and final. When it comes down to it, I'd sooner be moderately well off and libeled and alive than rich and vindicated and dead."

Harold hardly knew what to say to that. It was not a worldview to which he would have given houseroom for a moment. Yet clients were likely to do strange things, to panic without reason. You had to reassure them, keep them stable. . . .

Harold began, politely and reassuringly, to argue. To his shock, it did him no good. Richard was adamant. "I'm serious about it," he said. "We've got to let it go. I'm telling you, Harold, I want it dropped." And no matter how Harold argued and pleaded, and no matter how many ways he put the case, all Richard would say was, "We have to drop it."

Nearly an hour of this went by. "Come back tomorrow, and we'll discuss it again," Harold finally said.

"Harold," Richard said sadly, "in the words of my grandfather, 'What part of "no" didn't you understand?' We're dropping it. That's final. If you can't accept the instruction . . . I'll call Tollsworth."

Harold swallowed.

"Very well," he said at last. "I'll need your signature on some documents."

"I'll take care of that right now."

Harold swallowed one more time. He had hoped to be able to send Richard away on the pretext of needing time to prepare the virtual paperwork. But that apparently wasn't going to work.

He sat there frozen for a moment, then left the room. He asked his secretary to run every security check the firm could muster on the man in the virtual suite. And to log every word that was said in the boardroom—he didn't care if it was illegal. Then, after calling up the necessary documents himself, he returned. He dared not pass that particular aspect of the job on to his secretary. The minute she realized what he was doing, word would be all over the office, and Tollsworth would be in his office within minutes. There were several releases that he would need signed, and the main release, the document lesse mihi, for the High Court. Before he handed them over, he went through the arguments against what the client wanted one last time.

Richard produced his own pad, pulled out a gold and platinum stylus from his pocket. Harold hesitated. "You won't think again?" he asked.

Richard tapped his stylus against the pad and shook his head.

Harold let out a long breath and transferred the documents.

Richard signed the first one, paged to the next, signed that, paged on to the third. Signed it. Then he tapped the pad again, and the documents transferred themselves back to Harold's pad.

"Thank you," Richard said, and got up. "Thanks for everything, Harold. I know how hard you've tried, how hard the whole team has tried. It's just . . . time that it was over."

He stood up. Harold did, too. Richard came over and shook his hand, then walked out the door, shutting it behind him.

There was nothing Harold could do but go back to his office and prepare to transmit the documents. Naturally he had to call the Old Man in first.

Later, he preferred not to think about that particular interview. At the end of it, after he replayed his painful interview with the client an uncounted number of times for an increasingly hostile audience, the documents were transmitted, and Harold sat for a long time in the office, without turning on the lights, as outside, London darkened around him. It seemed a fitting expression of what was happening to his career, that just a couple of hours ago had seemed so bright.

What was far more terrible, though, was the next morning, when he came in—his head hurting badly enough already from the hangover of the night before—to see the shocked expression on his secretary's face. "Richard wants to talk to you on the secure link," she said.

Harold went down to the boardroom, cursing softly. He shut the door behind him, sat in the chair, lined his implant up, waited for the shiver of the background. Richard appeared in the chair opposite.

"Second thoughts?" Harold said, trying not to sound too bitter.

"About what? I thought I'd check in. Just got back from holiday. When do we go to appeal? Have they set a date?"

Harold's mouth fell open.

The next half hour's conversation took on a most surreal quality. Tollsworth came in to join it, and Harold heard language from him that he had never heard before. He would never hear it again, either, for by that afternoon Harold had been sacked—a scapegoat for a disaster of gigantic proportions. It seemed that Richard had never been on the link the previous day, that he had been off at some rich man's paradise in the Caribbean, doing virtual things in front of far too many witnesses, virtual and real, to be denied, and had only just come back. Whoever had been standing there, in Richard's body, using Richard's voice, and Richard's supposedly unbreakable security codes to get access to Tollsworth's virtual business space, had given them false instructions. And now Richard's lawsuit was over, for the documents dropping the case could not be unfiled. His case was—at least for the moment—lost, abandoned. The firm could, after testifying to the fraudulent instructions they'd received, get it reopened eventually, and might even get a trial scheduled again after a decade or so of legal wrangling. Tollsworth, Barrington-Smyth, and Hobart would still be a laughingstock, though. And at this very moment, the major national newspaper that had terribly and undeniably libeled his client was crowing its triumph over him from every front page, for naturally the assumption was that, since he had dropped the case, he must either have been guilty, or the case must have been judged unwinnable by his own law firm. Richard's satellite-components company, already suffering from much reduced share prices due to cuts in government defense spending and then due to the adverse publicity, took barely three weeks to fold. Richard's personal fortune, almost all of which he had pumped into his company, was gone in days. Within several months he was dead. Whoever had been impersonating him apparently had also seen his medical records, and about Richard's cardiac condition, at least, he had been speaking the truth.

A shudder went through Tollsworth, Barrington-Smythe, and Hobart. The firm's reputation suffered. Accounts were lost. There was discussion as to whether the firm would last more than another year. Tollsworth was getting old. All the senior partners were rich. There seemed no point in continuing, especially when people were suddenly taking their business to younger firms, ones that apparently had less trouble with technology. . . .

The Lord Chief Justice, in cooperation with the Home Office, began an investigation into the matter. None of this mattered to Harold. A week later he vanished from London, never to be heard from again. There were rumors he'd abandoned family, home, and hearth to go to the Caribbean and open a dive shop. But the fact that a firm like Tollsworth, Barrington-Smythe, and Hobart could be fooled was by far the most compelling gossip, discussed with some anxiety by men in hand-tailored suits across the globe. All over the planet, lawyers and barristers and solicitors began looking over their shoulders for one kind of ghost or another. . . .

Nearly a week and a half had gone by since Megan had spoken to James Winters, and she was going slightly nuts. She could rarely remember a summer when she had been so bored. This by itself bothered her, for Megan was almost never bored—there was just too much to do in life. Now, though, there wasn't even the distraction of school. Her best friend, Tina, was on vacation in Europe. Her brothers were out all day turning themselves into masses of bruises on various playing fields. Normally she would hardly have known or cared where they were, but now she half longed for the annoying distraction of their presence. Her mother was away half the time, off researching another story for *TimeOnline*, something inexplicable about the ozone layer and world air travel. Her father was buried in the den, working on the next book. Where Megan wanted to be, what she wanted to be working on, was Xanadu. Instead, about the most interesting thing there was for her to do was to go out back and watch her mother's thousands of tomatoes ripen.

It was a Saturday afternoon when she wandered into her dad's den for no reason other than to bother him. Rather to her surprise, he wasn't there. The books were there, though . . . all over the desks, all over the chair, sticking halfway out of the bookshelves in the way her dad left books he was working with so he could find them again in a hurry. One book was facedown on the seat of the implant chair. Another few were stacked in front of the computer's implant access reader, nearly blocking it as usual.

Megan wandered over to the desk and looked at the books

stacked on it. Her usual game was to pick the books up so carefully that, when she put them down again, one by one, her dad wouldn't know she'd been there. Then the point was to guess what they had to do with what he was working on . . . or, for that point, to figure out what he was working on in the first place. Her dad did not share his works in progress with other people. "Would you go out and stand on a street corner to get dressed?" Megan had once heard him say, rather in shock, to another writer who sent his work out to "readers" for advice before it was finished, and he maintained this attitude at home as well.

She had called him on this once, and he had admitted that what didn't work for some writers did work for others, but he still wouldn't let her see what he was doing until it was done.

She reached out and picked up the first book, being careful not to lose the page it was open to. Something from the library at Georgetown University, probably brought home by Paul: *Aztec Calendar Mythology*. She put up her eyebrows at that, laid the book open over her forearm, pages down, and picked up the next one. *The Agony and the Ecstasy*: Irving Stone's biography of Michelangelo. She draped that one over her arm, too. The third one was Rudyard Kipling's *Kim*. The fourth one was Clements's *Renaissance Swordsmanship*, followed by Pollard's *History of Firearms* and *The Guinness Book of Military Blunders*.

Megan put the last of these over her arm and was staring down at *The Dream King* and wondering harder than usual *What the heck is he doing?* when the phone next to her shrilled, and she nearly jumped out of her skin.

She hurriedly put the topmost of the books she was holding back down, in the position she had found it, and the phone rang once more, and then stopped. From down the hall Megan heard someone saying something muffled, and she grinned slightly. Her dad was in the bathroom and had picked it up there. He always claimed to hate the phone in the bathroom, which had been her mother's idea—"It always waits to ring while you're in there . . . haven't you noticed?"—but her dad wound up using it almost more than her mom did.

More muttering from down the hall. Very quietly Megan slipped out of the den and down the hallway to stand close to the bathroom door.

"Mmm-hmm. Yes. No, I hadn't. Frankly, I had hoped they wouldn't. The last session wasn't all that successful, and as pleasant as the surroundings were, I didn't see why they should waste their money, or my time."

That made Megan move a step or so closer to the bathroom door.

"All right," her father said, "convince me. You have five minutes." He sounded genial, but Megan knew that tone of voice. Whoever was on the other end of the phone—and she thought she knew—had his work cut out for him.

She stood there listening to her own heart beat, and listening to all the other house sounds, too, hoping desperately that none of her brothers would suddenly show up. At about the two-minute mark her father said, "Really."

He did not sound particularly convinced of anything. Megan let out the breath she had been holding.

A few moments later her father said, "James, excuse me. Could I have that again?"

A pause. Then her father said, "That would put an entirely different complexion on things, wouldn't it?"

Another pause.

"Well, they would still have to get in touch with me. They were supposed to do that last week, and I haven't heard from them. I assumed they'd decided to let it drop."

Megan swallowed.

"Oh," said her dad. "Oh. No, I guess not. Well . . . One thing I need from you. Some clarification about her role in this."

A long silence. Megan held her breath again.

"You're sure of that? Because if anything of the kind—"
Another long pause.

"No, of course not. It's just that I remember that last time. She cut it extremely close. I believe in public service as much as the next person . . . but this is my daughter we're talking about."

Silence. A long one. Megan let the breath out, but because she had to, not because she wanted to.

Finally there came a long sigh from inside the bathroom. "Well, look. If they match the deal from last time, all right. I can take my work with me. It's just that the place is full of distractions, and I'm not going to get as much done as I would here. By rights they should compensate me."

Another silence. "Yes. Yes, I'm sure she will. All right, so when do you—Really." A sudden laugh. "No, it's just nice to be in demand, I guess. All right, James. Yes. Thanks for calling. Goodbye."

The last words she could hardly hear, for at the sound of the laugh Megan knew what was happening, and she was already back in the den, stacking the books she had been holding back into their proper places and orientations. By the time the toilet flushed, and the faucets had run, and the door had opened, and her dad came moseying back into the den, Megan was standing by the computer chair, looking at the book that had been facedown on the seat. It was Michael Jackson's *Beers of the World*, and if she had been confused before about what her dad was working on, she was completely flummoxed now.

She looked up at him with the book in her hands. "What are you doing?" she said. "Come on, Daddy, tell me."

He raised his eyebrows. "You know, honey," her father said, "it's a wonderful thing to live in a place for a long time. You come to take it completely for granted. Its little quirks . . . its idiosyncrasies."

She looked at him with some bemusement, wondering what all this was supposed to be leading up to.

He was smiling slightly as he took *Beers of the World* away from her and sat down in the computer chair again, resting the book in his lap. "You've lived in this house all your life," he said, "and you know what? You don't even notice, anymore, the way that floorboard just to the right of the bathroom door creaks when you take your weight off it too fast."

Megan turned a color closely matching that which the tomatoes out in the back garden were now acquiring.

"I would suspect you of being behind that call just now,"

her dad said, "from James Winters, as if you don't know . . . except that he specifically said you had nothing to do with it. He's above prevaricating, so you're off the hook. But at the same time you have been talking to him . . . about Xanadu."

"About the problems there," she said, very carefully. "Yes."

He sighed and stretched his legs out. "I need to talk to you," he said, "about the dangers inherent in junketing. I know Net Force is primarily a law enforcement organization. But all public law enforcement organizations have political aspects to them. And when you—"

The phone shrilled again, and this time they both jumped. *Saved by the bell!* Megan thought, not much relishing the prospect of a lecture on anything while she was so excited. Her father got up hastily, went to the phone, picked it up.

"Hello," he said.

Another pause.

"Yes, Mr. Halvarson, how are you?" her father asked, with his eyebrows ascending straight up to where his hairline had been twenty years before. "Yes, a pleasure to speak to you, too. No, they told me you were away on business, I'm sorry to have missed the opportunity—"

He waved Megan out of the room. She went, restraining herself from the temptation to jump up and down for sheer joy as she did so. Her father pushed the door closed behind her.

Megan went into the kitchen to make herself tea, mostly as an exercise in keeping calm. By the time the water had boiled and the tea had brewed and she was halfway down the cup, her father wandered into the kitchen and sat down at the table.

"So?" Megan said, over her cup.

He gave her a look that was about half bemusement and half annoyance. "I want you to know," he said, "that I'm going to return to this paradise of hedonism and spend two weeks there for your sake."

"I'm sorry to make you suffer, Dad," Megan said, keeping her face as straight as she could under the circumstances.

"I'll bet," he said. But then his face cracked and let the

smile out, while maintaining the general look of bemusement. "I have to say," he said, "that my agent would probably have had strong words for me if I turned down the offer of a payment equaling the amount I'd get for a short novel, in return for two weeks of running the occasional seminar and otherwise just sitting around looking like I'm working on something."

"You were saying something about the dangers of junketing," Megan said, again very soberly.

Her dad gave her a look. "I'll get back to you on that," he said, "at intervals during this trip. Because, as you'll have guessed, you'll be there, too, disporting yourself. Or appearing to."

Megan grinned from ear to ear.

"Junketing aside," her father said, "I'm warning you. I know how serious you are about your Net Force work, and where you want to go with it. But if anything serious, anything really dangerous, starts to happen . . . I want to know about it first. That is the single condition under which I am sanctioning this little venture. If I get any sense that you're playing fast and loose in this regard, you and I are going to be on the next hopper home so fast your head will spin severely enough that you'll need to go in and have your vertebrae rethreaded."

Megan nodded. About this, she was not going to tease him. "I promise, Dad. I learned my lesson last time."

"Good. Then you'd better go make yourself up a packing list, because they're going to have a flyer here for us at nine tomorrow morning."

"Tomorrow!"

"And I've got to call your mother," said her dad, rubbing his forehead, "and find out when she can finally join us. And your brothers . . . who'll be all too delighted to have the house to themselves. I'm just hoping we don't come back to find nothing but a heap of smoking wreckage where the place used to be. And as for your mother's tomatoes . . . well, I guess the neighbors . . ."

The last part of this Megan heard only vaguely. She was already running down the hall to her room to start packing.

• • •

At eleven the next morning they were on the downward arc of their hopper's trajectory. The curvature of the Earth had just been lost to them, a brief sorrow to Megan. *That's as close as I'm likely to get to space, real space, for the immediate future anyway. . . .* But there was no telling what the later future might hold, and for the moment she had enough to think about as the blue of the northern Caribbean filled the hopper's windows, and she looked down at what the atlases called "New Bahama Island," and what the ads called Xanadu.

The place had nothing to do with the old Bahamas except that it was located in the same general latitude. It had been built on a seamount distantly associated with the Bahama chain, but not on one that was presently an island. "Or at least not in our present state of glaciation," as the Xanadu founder, Aaron Halvarson, had said in the promotional video.

The island had been built, mostly from scratch, in one of the more spectacular small feats of private engineering seen so far in this century. Using a combination of lava welding, millions of tons of processed construction rubble from the mainland, and many millions of tons more of refuse tailings reduced by plasma incineration to duraglass, the submerged seamount had been built up some six hundred feet to and above the surface of the ocean, the "mount" proper being extended some three hundred feet above sea level, and the base of the island mountain extended into a long curving lagoon structure reminiscent of Grand Bahama. The whole job had carefully been done far away from even the 150-mile fishing limit of the Bahamas, to prevent the possibility of awkward territorial claims by other countries after the property was completed. Indeed, some of the legal issues raised by the sudden appearance of new land in the middle of the ocean were still working their way through various national and international courts in the form of the so-called "Atlantis Suits," but for the moment the corporation funding Xanadu held all legal title to the land it had built up from a useless bump on the ocean floor, and had the powers of a sovereign government, even if it had not exactly tried to use many of them yet. Xanadu was primarily a commercial concern, but it had concluded a franchise-defense agreement with the Swiss government, "just in case." No one was sure exactly what the agreement involved besides sunny vacations for officers of the Swiss Landeswehr and Air Force. But there were recurring rumors that Mount Xanadu, like many mountains in Switzerland, was not exactly solid, and that there were things inside it that would make a potential attacker very unhappy.

Now, though, as Megan looked out of the window of the descending hopper at it all, she found it hard to make herself believe that this was anything but a natural environment. Several pods of dolphins were tracing a graceful arc into one of the harbors. In many places lush tropical forests came down almost to the edge of the water, the beaches edging them barely more than thin lines of peach or pink or white coral sand. On the inside curve of the island, though, the side protected from the prevailing easterly "trade winds," the beaches were broad, and as the hopper decelerated she could see people dotted here and there around them, stretched out on loungers or swimming in that amazingly blue water.

Megan smiled, as she had not been able to stop doing all morning. Part of her job was going to be to get out there and enjoy all that: the sun, the surf, all the rest of it. Travel, real travel as opposed to the virtual kind, had increasingly become the purview of the very wealthy as the twenty-first century progressed, and she planned to enjoy her unexpected chance at the good life for all it was worth. She had, though, also been deep in planning for the other work she had to do. Early yesterday afternoon Megan had found a great pile of information waiting for her in her workspace, in the form of encrypted E-mail, with a cover note from James Winters saying simply, "Read this. Destroy it." It had been more detailed information on all the previous data thefts and other crimes believed to be associated with the Xanadu site. The last brief she read, the story about the lawyer in London, had shocked her sufficiently that she had to just sit there and absorb the facts for some minutes before destroying the file and destructively rewriting the section of the computer's data solid that had contained it. *Whoever this is*, she thought, *they're profi-*

cient. And whoever it is, they're good at pretending to be someone they're not.

Rather than some kind of computer whiz buried in the background of the operation . . . could it be someone really closely involved with the "customers"? Or maybe two people, working closely together? One does the impersonations, one handles the software and hardware end of things . . . ?

She had tried, while they were finishing their packing the next morning, about an hour before the car came, to shoot this idea past her father and see what he thought of it. However, he had stopped her.

"Maybe it would be unwise for you to tell me, except generally, what you're doing," he said, closing a suitcase and fastening an ancient leather strap around it. "Or for me to comment. For three reasons. First, over the next couple of weeks I might accidentally let something slip to someone else that would be prejudicial to your business. Second, I might put some idea in your head that would distract or divert you from a better idea you might have yourself. And third, I might hear something that would so panic me that I'd ground you on the spot, pack you in one of your suitcases, and ship you home."

Megan had looked at him in surprise.

"Look," her father had said as the car started to drop down to the pad outside, "just be careful, and use your discretion. You must have some, or James Winters wouldn't give you the time of day. Speaking of which—"

He came up with the beat-up satchel in which he carried his "laptop" Net access computer, the one he used when going somewhere standard implant machines weren't available. Megan blinked.

"You're not going to need that where we're going, are you?"

"If it were mine," her father said, "no. Looks like mine, doesn't it? It should . . . the shell's the same. But the inside's a loaner."

"A loaner what? Is it from James Winters?"

"Close," said her father, though unnecessarily at the moment. "It's not for me . . . though it'll look that way. It's for

you to use." He slipped the "laptop" back into the bag.
"There's a secure satellite uplink installed in this, so you can
Net out or phone out without having to go through the Xanadu local Net systems. There are people who thought that
might be a good idea. It's been synched for your implant and
mine . . . no one else's."

" 'Close'?" Megan said. "You mean it's not from James
Winters?"

Her father grinned slightly. "I shouldn't tease you. From
Mark Gridley, actually. James Winters tells me that Mark has
expressed, uh, some interest in what's going on."

Megan grinned. She could imagine that only his father sitting on him forcefully had kept Mark from demanding to be
allowed to do what Megan was doing now—probably by
pointing out that sending the Net Force director's son to Xanadu would not be very low-profile behavior. "So this," she
said, guessing, "is a way that Mark can, uh, get in on the
action without actually being there."

"Virtually is actually enough, as far as the younger Gridley
is concerned," said Megan's father, looking a little wry as he
said it. "He's on standby to offer professional help, anyway.
Which strikes me as useful, since with systems as expert as
the Xanadu ones, I think you're likely to need it. One other
thing—"

He came up with a small handsome silvery oblong object
about a foot long and six inches wide. Megan reached out,
took it from her father, turned it over in her hands. It was a
"boom box": not one of the huge bulky brainblasters that
had first earned the name in the previous century, but one
with the new "solid radiation" speakers, which produced perfect surround sound from what appeared to be solid metal.
The controls were invisible until you stroked the metal under
which they hid, then the lights of them bloomed up out of
the brushed silvery finish.

Megan looked at her father again, resisting the temptation
to drool. "Tell me this is an early birthday present," she said,
"and not another loaner. Oh, please . . ."

He shook his head a little woefully. "Don't I wish, because
I would be borrowing it from you three times a week. It's

what it looks like, all right, but it's also a wide-spectrum anti-eavesdrop and antiscan device. That third 'toggle'—'' He passed a finger over the control surface until the controls showed again. ''Not that one, that's the volume. This one, that says 'graphic equalizer.' '' Her father looked slightly amused. ''Some frequencies are more equal than others, as some people will find if they try to listen to you while you have this turned on. If you've got private things to discuss with me, or someone else, keep this running. It generates 'blue noise' and various other useful things which I don't understand. But James Winters says your conversations will be safe with this. And it's your conversations that are mostly at issue here. I'm the overt part of this operation. The covert part is your business. Make sure you keep it that way . . . even from me, while we're there. They trust you. I trust you, too . . . but be careful.''

And he had packed up the ''laptop'' and the ''boom box'' and had said nothing more. Megan, picking up her bags at that point, had wondered briefly at such an enlightened point of view. *Is it possible*, she'd thought, *that our parents get smarter as we get older?*

The concept was intriguing, and only time would tell if it had any validity. Meanwhile, they had dropped almost all their acceleration now, and the hopper was flattening out onto the vectored thrusters for its landing.

The landing pad was surrounded at a safe distance by a circle of immense royal palms, the tops of which fluttered wildly like feather dusters in a windstorm as the hopper came down on its struts and rebounded a little, settling. The crew, who had been dancing attendance on them for the past hour, now set about opening the craft up, unsecuring the above-atmosphere seals. With a loud hiss the forward door a few seats ahead of Megan and her dad popped open, and warm tropical sunshine came pouring in, making the flight attendant wince and smile a little at it. A rampway came over from the side of the pad to meet them, and they and the three other people on the small private hopper, all staff in the Caribbean-blue Xanadu uniform, got off.

Megan's attention was divided between paying attention to

how she walked down the ramp and trying to get a view around her. The burning blue and white of the day was dazzling, edged on nearly all sides by tropical green. Here and there a glimpse of the sea was visible through the trees, and off to the west of them Mount Xanadu loomed over everything, lush and green, with huge waterfalls rushing down its sides, from this distance visible only as static angular stripes of white. Around the landing pads were flower beds; a parking lot for a cluster of small, flat-decked wheeled vehicles; and a large number of people in Xanadu uniforms who were making their way out to the hopper to unload it.

Megan stepped down off the ramp behind her father, stood there, and took a long breath of the warm, salty air. *This is absolutely terrific*, she thought—and then someone tried to pull her briefcase-shoulderbag off her shoulder.

Megan just managed to keep her body from reacting to that, with unfortunate results for whoever was pulling on the bag. She turned and found a little man in a neat blue uniform with crossed keys embroidered on his collar, who smiled and said, "I'll take that for you, Miss O'Malley."

"Uh, no, it's okay, I usually—"

"Oh, Miss O'Malley, we can't have guests carrying their own luggage. What would people say?"

He smiled at her winningly. Megan knew a lost argument when she heard one, and she ducked a little to let the man slip the bag off her shoulder. Away he went with it, and as she turned around to say something to her father, she saw that he, too, was now empty-handed and looking amused.

"That happened last time, too," he said to her in a low voice as they followed their guide away from the landing pad. "I have a feeling most people who come here just drop their bags and expect them to be caught before they hit the ground."

"Mmm," Megan said, and followed him. One of the staff people was beckoning them through an arch-shaped pergola in a wall covered with white climbing roses. On the far side was a series of long curving ramps leading down to a wide blue lagoon completely surrounded by beaches of black sand, and there appeared to be a wave generator operating at the middle of the lagoon, for waves were slipping gently up the shoreline all around and sliding back again. As the waves receded, the sand turned silver under the sun, then tarnished to matte black as the water slipped out to the lagoon again.

The ramps led around the lagoon on both sides to what appeared to be a reception center. Parked off to their right, under the shade of a cluster of royal palms, was a group of small vehicles like golf carts—except that golf carts rarely had the kind of perfectly hide-matched leather upholstery these did, the kind you might expect to find inside a Rolls-Škoda. One of the staff standing by these carts came over to them and said, "Please come this way, Mr. O'Malley, Miss O'Malley . . ."

They got into one of the little carts, and a Xanadu staff member drove them down the path to the broad graveled space in front of the reception center. After that it was "I'm Joel, your driver. Right this way, Mr. O'Malley" this, and "This way please, Miss O'Malley" that, until Megan was tempted to start giggling every time she heard it. The reception center itself was a wide, Greek-pillared circular area, open to the sky, but Megan had just enough time, as they were whisked through, to see the wide slot in the pediment the columns supported. Probably the roof would come irising out of it in case of bad weather.

"Now," said Joel-Their-Driver, "this is where you come if you care to socialize with the other guests while you're here. You should feel free to come down here and see us if you have any problems with your facilities while you're here, any problems at all concerning your stay. Or just call us and we'll send someone around to your villa. Our operations center is in the building behind main reception. You should feel free to stop by any time you like—each guest is entitled to a tour of the facility. As many as they like, in fact; just call and let us know you're coming. There are twelve restaurants on the island. We'll be passing three of them on the way to your villa, and any time you feel inclined to have a snack, either someone will come from room service with whatever you like, or you can call for a jitney and we'll drive you around to whichever restaurant takes your fancy. All of them are open for lunch and dinner, five of them serve breakfast, and two are open twenty-four hours a day.'' Joel grinned. ''I recommend The Deli, myself. We do a really nice pastrami-cured salmon.''

He went on in this vein for several more minutes as he drove around the eighteenth hole of an extremely scenic golf course, and past it through what appeared to be a small rain forest. Megan was noticing the terrain a little less than she had been a few minutes before. Her stomach had awakened abruptly at the mention of pastrami. *A sandwich of any kind would go down pretty well right now,* she thought. But then, she had been too excited to eat breakfast, and possibly that had been wise. The high-injection trajectory hoppers had affected her badly once or twice before.

How long is it going to take us to get where we're going? she wondered. ''This place is really big,'' Megan said. ''I thought it was much smaller, somehow.''

''Half the size of Manhattan Island, Miss O'Malley,'' said Joel. ''And in fact there's a fair amount of Manhattan underneath us here. We took all their garbage for the better half of a year to process into the duraglass and synthalava that was used to build the island's substrate. We've kept the guest quarters fairly close to the central buildings, though. We'll be at your villa in about three minutes.''

Did he hear my stomach rumble? Megan wondered. It wouldn't have surprised her if a place like this trained its staff to be alert for such signs.

At any rate, it was more like a minute and a half. Their driver sped up somewhat. They came out of the rain forest into an area that was more like rolling parkland, all very trim and domesticated-looking broad lawns, plantings of palms and conifers obviously designed to create little pockets of privacy. Beyond it all lay the bright blue line of the sea, with glimpses of the beach—this one a sparkling white sweep of sand—showing through the trees.

''Your villa is down this way,'' said Joel, turning the jitney to the left, into a little paved lane overhung with big old eucalyptus trees. ''One of our choicer areas, I have to say . . . nice and private. If you want to come 'inland' without calling a jitney, there's a public transport that stops at this junction every ten minutes. And of course there are bicycles up at the villa.''

They came out from under the eucalyptuses into a clearing in which was set a white building bigger than Megan's house, apparently designed by someone who had caught the Neo Deco bug. Each of the two main wings was a wide, broad-based cylinder with a railed observation deck on top. They met in a slimmer, taller cylinder that housed the front door and had its own tower-top deck atop it. "You get a great view from there," said Joel.

"This isn't the same villa I stayed in last time," Megan's father said, looking around in surprise.

"No, sir. We match each villa to our guests' needs. Since you brought the young lady along, we feel you'll probably find this one more to your liking."

The drive changed from dark paving to white gravel in the open space in front of the villa. Joel stopped the jitney in front of the door. "Let me open it up and give you the keys," said Joel, "and I'll give you a quick tour. Your luggage should be here already and up in your rooms. Any problems, let me know, I'll fix them. . . ."

"I'm going to walk around the back, Dad," Megan said, getting out. She had already spotted the house's private beach, out behind it, and something else—a glimpse of another white building through the trees.

"Those are your neighbors, Miss O'Malley," Joel called after her, catching her glance in that direction. "They're the only ones down this lane. They got here a couple of days ago . . . you can meet them at the reception center tonight, if you like."

Megan waved at him and wandered on around the path that led behind the house. There was a wide patio back there, overflowing with tropical plants in beds and containers. Another graveled path led past a heavily landscaped swimming pool terrace, and then down to the beach.

Megan sighed at the sight of it and walked down past the palm trees that partially screened the view. She had never lived or stayed anywhere that hadn't had reasonably easy access to the ocean, but this was easier than usual. Burning blue sky met hot blue sea in a horizon that almost wasn't even a visible line—only a few bright white clouds, a long way off, differentiated air from water. It was all incredibly beautiful and restful-looking.

And I have to work on stuff while I'm here. It's not fair! But then she laughed at herself. The work was the reason she was here in the first place.

She turned and made her way back toward the house. The French doors to the patio were standing open, and she made her way in through them and found herself in a living room practically the size of the whole first floor of her house. It had a huge fireplace—though why anyone would want or need a fireplace when the temperature outside was mostly around eighty degrees all year long, Megan couldn't imagine. The fireplace was loaded with beautifully split hardwood, artistically arranged in a configuration that Megan suspected would light the minute you put a spark to it . . . probably because the people who would be here would expect it to do that, she thought. Off to the right side of it, as she faced the front of the house, was a dining room with a marble-topped table easily big enough to seat twenty. She saw a door past that. *The kitchen?* she thought.

Her dad was coming down the stairs. "Joel's gone on his way," he said. "I thought I might get a glass of something cold and locate enough food and water to enable me to explore the rest of this place."

"Not a bad idea," Megan said, heading for that door off the dining room. Peering through it, she found a room about the size of her own living room, completely done in the sleekest possible black glass and matte bronze. The appliances were sunk discreetly into walls or hidden behind black glass doors. Taking a look at the controls for a few of them, Megan began to suspect that some of these machines were smarter than some people she went to school with. "Look at this stuff," she said to her dad as he came in behind her. "I'd be terrified to cook in here. It's all so shiny. . . ."

"I wonder if anyone actually does bother to cook," her father said, "considering the reputation of the restaurants in this place. Well, all I want is some soda water at the moment.''

''I'll get it.'' She went to open the refrigerator. ''That at least they must have. I'd kill for a baloney sandwich at the moment, but I doubt they'd—''

Megan's mouth dropped open as the contents of the refrigerator registered. They were identical to those of her fridge at home this morning. *Except that it hasn't been stripped bare by one of the four resident members of the U.S. Olympic Eating Team,* she thought. ''Daddy, do you believe this?''

He looked over her shoulder while heading for the cupboards to start glancing through them. ''Oh. Interesting. I guess they must have queried the recent inventories on the fridge and pantry at home.'' He grinned as he got a glass down from one of the cupboards. ''We may have to tell them to cut back a little, seeing that the Four Horsemen of the Apocalypse aren't here to help us empty it.''

''I was just thinking that. . . .'' She reached in, got the baloney and the mustard out, then shut the door and went off to see about some bread. The ''bread box'' was a glass-doored cupboard near the fridge that appeared to have been adapted from some kind of humidor, and displayed the inside temperature and relative humidity in the glass of the door.

Megan got out the bread, took a couple of slices out of the wrapper, and put the loaf away again, at which point the humidor got frantically busy adjusting its humidity again. She made her sandwich, found a plate to put it on—this place was so obsessively clean that she would have felt too guilty to put the sandwich down on a table or a counter—and wandered out of the kitchen.

She went back through the living room and glanced around. Off to the right side was a small hallway where Megan suspected there was a bathroom. She wandered down, looked in.

Her mouth dropped open, and she closed it again. She was going to have to watch that, lest people here get the idea that she was some kind of mouth-breather. *Or that I'm not used to this kind of thing,* she thought. *Bathroom indeed.* It had a toilet and a bidet in clear glass stalls, a tub large enough for her and about ten of her biggest friends, a steam cabinet, another wooden door that she thought was probably a sauna, a shower that had so many unfamiliar nozzles and apertures that it looked like it might double as some kind of rest room facility for alien beings, and a pure white marble floor—not tiled marble, but a single seamless slab of the real stuff.

She wandered over to the glass stall surrounding the toilet, wondering what use it was. Its door stood open. She swung it shut, and it latched itself . . . and the glass of the stall opaqued, went frosty, in a breath's space.

Megan blinked, pulled the stall door open. The glass went clear.

She headed out, closing the bathroom door behind her. "Daddy?" she said, and bit into her sandwich as she headed up the wide spiral staircase.

"Yes, honey?" he said from the kitchen.

"I am never leaving here," she said.

"That's nice, honey."

Megan made her way up the stairs and ambled around on the second floor, looking into doorways. There were five bedrooms in their villa. Whether they had been given one bigger than the last one because of this particular job, or whether their hosts thought the guests here might get tired of just one bedroom and prefer a different one after a night or two, Megan had no idea. The bedrooms were, to put it mildly, palatial. They all had tiny kitchen niches, computers with huge comfortable access-lineup chairs of the newest make, bathrooms of at least the same complexity and luxury as the one downstairs, and stunning views out over the lagoon on one side, or the Atlantic on the other. The beds were big enough to need their own ZIP codes, and thirteen-digit ones at that. The carpets had pile so deep that you were in danger of sinking into them without a trace, Megan thought, if you stood in the same place too long.

"Amazing," she muttered between bites of her sandwich as she moved from room to room. Down at the end of the hall she came to a door that at first she thought was going to be another bedroom, maybe the master. On opening the door, though, she simply stood and stared.

It was the biggest, sleekest, most modern-looking computer suite she had ever seen or heard of.

The room was a huge ellipse, with the access chair at one node of the ellipse and the access computer at the other. She went over to it where it sat in pride of place, and simply stood there shaking her head. Here was an IndexBlue Netset, a piece of machinery that easily cost as much as a custom race car . . . as well as one of the BodyMatch access chairs that could give you a whole-body massage as well as doing the usual internal muscle stimulus, to keep you from cramping up during those long virtual sessions.

Megan went over to the Netset and touched its query pad, getting it to read out its specs, while her dad went by in the hall, making his way among the bedrooms as she had done. "Oh, this one's mine, I guess." The sounds of various drawers being opened then followed. "They've unpacked for me," he added. "I hope you didn't have anything in your luggage you didn't want looked at, honey, because someone's seen it now."

She shook her head and left the Netset computer alone as her dad came down the hall again. "Look at all of this!"

He glanced in through the doorway. "Nice, isn't it? You could get a lot of work done in a place like this. If you ever came in from outside . . ."

"I can't resist," Megan said. She sat down in the chair, lined her implant up with it experimentally. She was curious to see what their interface acted like. The feeling like an aborted sneeze—

—and she was standing at the top of her amphitheater, looking down at Saturn.

Her eyes widened at that. *They've got all my profiles in here!* "Daddy," she said aloud, "did you give them my access area authorizations?"

"Nope," he said from out in the real world. Apparently they had a repeater installed in here as well. "You did, when you filled out and signed that questionaire they sent you. Always read the small print, honey."

"Oh, I read it. But I just thought they meant they were going to redirect my E-mails and virt-mails for me."

"They have everything the way you like it?"

"If you mean, the way it is at home, yeah."

I'm not sure I like this, Megan thought, looking around. *Granted, the Net server where I keep my workspace is a public one, but* . . . She broke the interface, resolving to take a closer look at the encryption on the files she preferred to keep private. Somebody here was very, very good with computers, virtualia, and the Net . . . and she was beginning to wonder if this was the source of the trouble Xanadu had been having.

"They guarantee you complete service," her father said. "It kind of surprised me, too, when I got here the first time and found they had all my preferred software, customized to my exact tastes installed, and access to my workspace. But I don't keep really important things in there anyway."

Megan snorted at this. In some ways her father was an incorrigible Luddite. This was one of the reasons why his den was always littered with little scribbled-up pieces of paper, which he sometimes lost, instead of files secured and stored away in the machine where he could find them afterward. And he was a fiend about printouts. The filing cabinets in the office were stuffed full of pages and pages of old books, articles, research material, and heaven knew what else. Then again, the thought of a storage failure in the machine did not much bother her dad, whereas Megan's mother would go pale at the very mention of a lost file or a power outage in the middle of a save.

Now, though, Megan was feeling a little pale herself, wondering exactly when the Xanadu staff had tapped into her system. Before she got the mail from James Winters? After? *I've got to have a glance through there later and see if there are any timestamps that suggest when they lifted my files. Slick little monsters* . . .

"Dad," she said, "this is a lot to take in all at once. So I'm not going to think about it. I'm going to go out to the beach again."

He chuckled. "Right. I could use a shower. Then maybe some lunch?"

"Sounds good."

She went down the stairs and out the French doors to the

back again, and once more wandered down the gravel path to the beach. This particular beach—she'd seen beaches on the island ranging from black to pink to beige to white as she'd flown in—was that perfect soft white coral sand—not the harsh white quartz sand you got along most of the Washington-area beaches—and completely clean, not studded with broken clamshells and slivers of glass and less wholesome things, like most of the public beaches she knew. *Probably someone comes and rakes this at night*, she thought, *and sifts out anything that floated in to mess it up.*

She walked along it for a few minutes, slowly, just staring out at the blue. This was really all idyllic. But she could not get out of her mind that London lawyer, Harold Hyphen-Hyphen-Whatever, his life ruined, abandoning everything he'd ever known and disappearing. And his poor client, dead and dishonored. *Someone here was responsible for that*, Megan thought. *Tomorrow morning, first thing . . . it'll be time to start finding out who.*

"What are you doing on our beach?" an unfamiliar voice suddenly said.

Megan whirled and saw a teenage boy standing there. He was about her height, a little heavy but not overly so. Some of it at least was muscle. Dark hair, dark eyes, a frowning kind of face: frowning at her, at the moment.

Megan glanced around her to make sure of where she was, then turned to him. "I'm sorry," Megan said. "This is behind our villa. This is our beach."

The kid opened his mouth and then shut it again, as if he would have liked to argue the point but couldn't find any way to do so. "Well, stay off ours," he said.

"I didn't have any plans to invade," Megan said, "and frankly, why would I bother?"

"Because my dad's the third richest man on the planet," said the kid, "and everybody tries. Who's your dad?"

Oh, boy, Megan thought, *here we go. Not "My name is, what's yours,"* not *"What brings you here . . ."*

"He's a writer," Megan said.

"Oh," said the kid, in a tone of voice that suggested writers were some kind of bottom-feeder. "What's his name?"

"R. F. O'Malley," Megan said.

"Never heard of him," the kid said.

It helps to know how to read, Megan thought, and then repressed that reply. Instead she adapted one of her father's responses, which could be either ironic or rude when he used it, but wasn't so bad for her. "Just make sure you do before you die," she said, "or you'll have missed the whole point of being on the planet. And who are you, exactly?"

"Wim Dorfladen."

"Ah. And this is a good thing?" said Megan, who was not beyond being rude herself when the occasion seemed to call for it.

"Better than being some writer's kid that nobody ever heard of," said Wim.

"I'm sure you think so," said Megan. "Well, now that we've gotten that straightened out, get off my beach before I flatten you."

He sneered at her and took a step forward. "You couldn't—uhh!"

She flattened him. It was the foot-sweep that her brother had tried to use on her the morning before, but she did it so fast that Wim never saw what had happened to him—he simply found himself sitting in the sand. "Hey, you've got to watch this sand, it's slippery sometimes," Megan said. "You need some help?"

He stared in surprise at the hand she was holding out to him, got up, looking at Megan with complete confusion, and just turned his back and walked off.

Stuck-up little creep, Megan thought. *And this is one of our neighbors? So much for Paradise.*

She ambled back up to the house again, where she went upstairs and found her father still fully clothed, standing in his own suite's bathroom and staring at the shower cabinet in complete bemusement. "I've seen less complicated setups in nuclear facilities," he said. "This isn't the same setup they had in my villa the last time I was here. How many of these do you think emit water? And how many of them are likely to spit live steam and cook me like a lobster?"

"I was wondering about that earlier," Megan said, but she

was wondering about something else now. "Dad, you don't suppose they'd let us change villas—" Then she made a face, for it sounded stupid even asking. *As if I can't handle him. As if I haven't handled him already.* "Never mind."

"All right. But why do you ask?"

"The kid next door is an incredible snot," she said, "and his father is the third richest man on the planet, or so he claims. Possibly we could have done better as far as neighbors were concerned."

"Oh, well," her father said, plainly concentrating on something else. "If that's all . . . Does this thing have a user's manual, I wonder?"

Megan snickered and went to help him find it.

3

While her dad was showering, Megan rummaged around the villa a little more. She knew that the Xanadu visitor's guide was available online, but there was also a book version that she found on one of the bedside tables. Despite the proliferation of electronic texts, she still loved the feel of a real bound volume in her hands. The book was nearly as thick as one of her father's novels—the "hard" copy of one, anyway. Like all authors, most of her father's books came out electronically; but he considered himself a throwback and still insisted on getting his author's copies of each title in printed and bound editions. Inside the gilt-trimmed tooled leather cover of the visitor's guide was everything one could want to know about the resort, carefully thumb-indexed along the gold-leafed page edges and sorted alphabetically by topic. She leafed through it and made mental notes on this and that.

After a while her dad came out, wearing the thickest bathrobe Megan had ever seen, and looking as pink as one of the lobsters he had mentioned. "This thing tonight is sort of a captain's table kind of affair," she said, getting up and chucking the book onto her father's bed. "But you don't have to get really dressed up if you don't want to, it says."

"Good, because I won't," he said, and vanished into the walk-in closet. "You might want to dress a little, though."

"Me? Why?"

"Protective coloration?" her father said.

Megan thought about that, and then went off to see about implementing it. About half an hour later they met downstairs. Her father looked her up and down. He was wearing beige linen pants and a white shirt, no tie. Megan had put on a flowing white dress, mini in front and maxi in back, that covered her pretty much completely, but (she thought) also suggested to the intelligent viewer that white did not necessarily mean total innocence.

Her father gave her a hard look but made no comment. He locked up the villa, and they headed off down the lane, through lengthening evening shadows and balmy air. About halfway down the lane, he looked at her. " 'Dorfladen'?" he said suddenly. "Was that the name?"

"Yeah."

"Did he mention a first name?"

"Not for his dad. The kid's name is Wim," Megan said as they came to the corner with the path that led toward the central reception facility.

Her father put his eyebrows up. "Well," he said after a moment, "he's maybe the fourth richest man on the planet. Unless the standings have changed in the last couple of months. God knows, I don't pay attention to such things."

Megan had her own opinions about that. "What does he do?"

"He makes money," her father said.

"I kind of thought so," Megan said. "Otherwise he wouldn't be here."

"No," her dad said, "that's not what I mean. He's a broker, essentially. He buys things cheap and sells them dear. Companies, currencies, you name it. He started with a company he founded, then started a few more, then sold them off, and got seriously into the business of corporate acquisitions—occasionally, into 'raiding,' buying companies that didn't want to be bought, selling them to people who wanted them, taking a profit off the top." Megan's father frowned.

"He's not some kind of crook, is he?" Megan said.

"Huh? Oh, no, honey. What he does is all perfectly legal."

Her father walked some ways farther before saying, "Call it an irrational prejudice on my part. If I were going to be rich, I'd rather do it by inventing something or making something that was of use to people . . . something that hadn't been there before . . . than by taking the result of other people's work, whether they like it or not, and auctioning it off to the highest bidder. But people like Dorfladen, if this man is who I think he is, don't actually make anything new. They make their fortunes by standing on the shoulders of other people. Or, sometimes, by kicking other people's feet out from under them."

Megan blushed slightly.

"As I said, an irrational prejudice," her dad said. "His response to that opinion would probably be something along the lines of 'If you're so superior—why haven't you found a moral way to be rich?' And by his lights, that would make perfect sense." He shrugged.

Behind them came the faint electric whine of one of the little Xanadu jitneys, the "public transit."

"You want to ride the rest of the way?" her father said.

Megan smiled slightly. "Just this once, yeah," she said, "because probably everybody else will, and if we show up walking, they'll all talk."

The jitney came by and slowed up, seeing them. "Going our way, son?" said Megan's dad.

"You bet, Mr. O'Malley, Miss O'Malley," said the driver. "Hop right in."

They did. "You've all seen mug shots of us now, I bet," Megan said, leaning over the driver's shoulder from the seats behind him to read his name tag. "Mihaul? Is that how to say it?"

"Close enough." He was a slim redheaded guy, and he gave Megan an amused sideways look as he drove. "Of course we all know what you look like. We knew two days ago. But besides that," he said, slowing down to take a curve, "some of us read."

"Aha," said Megan's father. "Willingly? Or is that part of the mug shot process, too?"

Mihaul laughed. "Not a chance. I read *Night's Black Engineers* the first time when I was eleven."

Megan's dad winced. "Please, don't, you'll just make me feel old."

"And about twenty times since then."

"That's all very well," her father said, "but how many of the new books have you read?"

Megan sat back and let her dad do the famous-writer thing while she measured the distance they were traveling by eye and second-count. It looked as if it would routinely take her about ten minutes to get up to the main facility from the villa on foot—probably about six minutes on one of the villa's bikes. She was going to have to make some friends inside there over the next few days. Her main problem was that Mr. Winters had told her to keep the reason she was at Xanadu secret. Possibly nobody but her father knew why she was there. If somebody knew, the odds of the news getting to the person or persons she was trying to identify were entirely too good. She was going to have to feel her way through this, watching and listening carefully to see who seemed too interested in her presence, or alternatively, not interested enough. *I've got my work cut out for me. But then, I asked for this job. . . .*

They drew up in front of the main reception area. It was astonishingly changed from the way it had seemed just a few hours before—lit up brilliantly from inside, with music floating out into the growing dusk, some kind of chamber orchestra playing restrained but energetic swing. They got down out of the jitney, and Mihaul said, "I'll be back this way every so often, Mr. O'Malley, Miss O'Malley, if you decide to call it a night before midnight."

They nodded, waved to him, and then went in through the columned portico. Inside, the semicircular reception counters they had glimpsed earlier in the day were completely transformed. One of them was now a bar about fifty feet long, and another had become a buffet about twice that length, and both were manned with white-coated staff managing heroic amounts of food and drink.

Past the buffets was what looked like a huge circular dance

floor surrounded by tables and sofas and comfortable chairs.
A few people were dancing, more people were sitting and
chatting, and a man in white tie, with long blond hair and
one of those beautifully chiseled Scandinavian faces, was
making his way from table to table, pausing to talk to people.
He looked up, saw them, and came over toward them. "Mr.
O'Malley. Miss O'Malley—"

He shook Meg's father's hand, then Meg's. "Mr. Aaron
Halvarson, I presume," her father said.

The blond man laughed. "Presume anything you like, but
don't *Presume Me Guilty*," he said. Megan's father groaned
in an amused way. It was the title of one of his earlier mysteries, the one that had won him the "Edgar" and gotten him
into a three-year-long argument with the lead book critic of
the *New York Times*.

"I'm sorry," Halvarson said. "That one must be getting
old."

"I believe it appears in cave paintings," Meg's dad said.
"Mr. Halvarson, my daughter, Megan."

"Charmed," Halvarson said, and actually bent over her
hand and kissed it. Megan gave him just a fraction of a nod,
and enough of a smile to let him know she appreciated it.

"Are you going to be assisting your father with his seminar
work?" Halvarson said.

"Not if I can avoid it," Megan said. "I'm going to be
assisting your 'virtualia' people with their quality control by
getting into every scenario they'll let me near."

"Ahh. Are you into software or hardware, then?"

"Software by preference," Megan said, "but I test hardware when it comes my way."

"Indeed. Well, I'm sure we can arrange something like that
for you. Meanwhile, come meet some of my staff. And some
of your fellow guests, of course."

"How many are we on the island this week?" her father
said as Halvarson led them off to one side, where there was
another buffet and a smaller bar.

"Twenty-six guests," Halvarson said, "fourteen of whom
have pavilions in various stages of design. We're almost at
capacity. This is our busy season. Another two guests come

in tomorrow, and then no more for a few days. Please, can I give you something to drink? Something to snack on?''

Megan glanced at the buffet table over to the left and saw a Lalique crystal bowl the size of a basketball, full of ice and with another smaller bowl nested inside it, full of about a pound or so of caviar. Next to it, beyond the chopped onion and chopped egg and blinis and sour cream, was a plate containing a cold lobster the size of a small child, without a scrap of shell on it, and completely perfect down to the tips of the claws. ''How do they do that?'' Megan said.

Halvarson glanced over at the lobster as if noticing it for the first time. ''You mean, get the shell off it without damaging the rest? You know, I've never asked. If you'd like to find out, I'll make an appointment for you with Catering.''

''It can wait,'' Megan said. ''I wouldn't mind some mineral water.''

''Champagne for me,'' her father said. ''Work starts tomorrow. Tonight, folly and excess.''

He'll get heartburn, Megan thought, but said nothing. When their glasses came, they each toasted their host and drank, and then Halvarson said, ''My deputy director is with us tonight. Come meet her.''

They wandered over to a table where several people were sitting and talking intently. Two of them were young men. One was a tall fair young woman. All three glanced up as Halvarson approached, and the young woman stood.

''Mr. O'Malley, Miss O'Malley,'' Halvarson said, ''may I present Norma Wenders, our deputy director.''

The tall fair lady to whom he had introduced them bowed slightly. ''I'm very pleased to meet you,'' she said, and gave Megan a long, cool smile. Megan thought she recognized that expression. She had seen teachers who wore it while a student's parent was within range. More or less, it said, Don't make my life difficult. If you do, you'll have more trouble than it'll be worth to you.

''Norma supervises Operations,'' said Halvarson, ''and generally rides herd on this place when I have to be out playing the salesman.''

''He's overstating my case somewhat,'' said Ms. Wenders,

giving Megan's dad an amused look. "The staff are the real workers around here. I only get to take the credit, though sometimes I look over their shoulders briefly."

The look on her face suggested that having one's shoulder looked over by this ice maiden was probably not a delightful experience. *Wonderful,* Megan thought. *This is the person I'm going to have to deal with while I'm trying to make friends with the Ops people.*

"These are the real workhorses around here," Ms. Wenders said, indicating the two young men she was sitting with, both of whom were wearing tuxes and were apparently making a serious attempt to look elegant, even though, Megan thought privately, they mostly still looked like nerds in tuxes. "Len MacIlwain, he's our security and implementation officer, and Nasil Rajasthani, he's in charge of pavilion realization."

They both ducked their heads a little to Megan and her dad. "Mr. O'Malley is running the writers' workshop for the next couple of weeks," Halvarson said, "Megan is interested in virtual realization."

"Come on by," said MacIlwain, "and we'll give you the fifty-cent tour."

"Splurge," said Rajasthani. "Give her the dollar one."

"What, and spend money?" MacIlwain said. The two of them grinned at each other.

Ms. Wenders gave them a look. "If only that healthy attitude could be something we hear from you two when it comes time every year to buy new equipment."

"Got to stay on the cutting edge," said MacIlwain.

"Push out the boundaries of the envelope," said Rajasthani.

"Somehow all their conversations wind up sounding like something to do with a stationery store," Halvarson said in a quiet aside to Megan. "Let's move along a little. . . . There are a couple of other people here you should meet."

After politely disentangling them from his staff, he led them off around the room, and Megan did her best to file away the names against the faces they were introduced to. It was a problem—partly because she had never been good at being given large numbers of names all at once, but also because, though the clothes and jewelry of the people they were meeting were splendid, sometimes almost staggeringly expensive, their faces seemed to lack something. It was as if many of the people weren't enjoying themselves, particularly. Oh, they were smiling, and joking and laughing, and when you were introduced to them, they smiled and were pleased to meet you . . . but Megan noticed that it didn't seem to last—that often, when you were halfway around the room, you might glance back and see those same faces, in an unguarded moment, gone grim, or slack, as if nothing much mattered. Another person would come along, another stimulus, and they would brighten, but it seemed temporary.

Now that makes no sense. These people are here on vacation. They're planning to have a good time. What's wrong here? Megan thought. *It's got to be too simplistic to put that all down to 'money doesn't bring you happiness.' Whether or not it does, it sure makes life a lot easier, and at the very least, a lot of these people should be more relaxed than they look. Why aren't they?*

It was a question to which she suspected no answers were going to be forthcoming any time soon. *Maybe I'm just tired,* Megan thought. *It has been kind of a long day.* And always buzzing at the back of her mind was the thought of the work she was going to have to start tomorrow. She wasn't sure where to begin. That was part of the trouble. *I'm going to have to start coming up with some ideas.*

She found herself standing behind her dad a moment later, being introduced to yet one more guest—and suddenly her attention snapped fully into focus, for she had seen this face somewhere. He was not a very tall man, maybe no taller than Megan was herself—a little stocky, broad-shouldered, with salt-and-pepper hair and a face that was all laugh lines, the eyes drooping a little at the corners. Noticeably, he stood up when they came over.

Halvarson smiled a little as he told the man Megan's and her father's names. "Mr. O'Malley, Ms. O'Malley," he said, "Jacob Rigel."

"Wow," Megan said, and stuck her hand out. "Call me

Megan. I've always admired your work with the space jeeps. I'm really pleased to meet you.''

"Jacob, then," he said. They shook, and he and her father did, too. Rigel looked at Megan with mild interest. "I'm not used to being treated as such a celebrity," he said. "Are you with the media or something?"

Megan laughed and sat down. "No. Well, maybe, yeah. My dad and mom both write."

"And you do—what?"

"I'm professionally nosy," Megan said, since it was true enough.

"It's an honorable profession," Rigel said. "All the really good things ever invented started as either daydreams or nosyness." He looked at her father with amusement. "As I suspect you know, if you're the O'Malley I think you are. The mysteries?"

"That's right."

Rigel grinned. "Maybe we can get together for a chat sometime during the week. I'm not going to last much longer here tonight. I'm three time zones out of place at the moment."

"My pleasure," Megan's father said, "any time you please."

Halvarson led them off toward the back of the party area, toward a group of small tables near the part of the reception area that gave onto the big garden out in the back. "These are the last introductions for the evening," he said as they came up to the tables. Two people were sitting there—a big broad-shouldered man, with a wide face, hair thinning on top, filling his black tie jacket as if he had been poured into it, and a teenage boy.

Megan swallowed and tried not to have it show.

"Arnulf Dorfladen," said Halvarson, "may I present Mr. Robert O'Malley and his daughter, Megan. Mr. O'Malley, a writer of some renown, has kindly agreed to teach a writing workshop for us."

"Is that so? I doubt I'll have the time to attend." The big man nodded an acknowledgment to his host, looked her father up and down, then gave Megan a glance that summed her up and dismissed her in about a second. His eyes were as cool, in their way, as Norma Wenders's had been, but her expression had at least suggested that Megan might have some worth. In Dorfladen's case, she saw herself being labeled *Immature Female, No Commercial Value.*

"*Gruss Gott*, Herr Dorfladen," her father said, and gave the man the slightest bow. Megan glanced up in surprise.

"*Gruss Gott*," said Dorfladen, looking at her father with surprise at least equal to Megan's. "*Herr* . . . O'Malley. Is my accent then so familiar?"

"To one who has visited the south often enough, yes," her father said, and added a phrase in what Megan assumed was some odd variant of German.

Dorfladen actually laughed. "So I see," he said. "A pleasure to meet you. Here also is my son, Wim." He glanced now at Megan as if he were reassessing her. "Maybe you two will keep each other out of trouble, yes?"

Not a chance in a hot place, Megan thought. "We've met," Megan said, being careful to keep any shade of further meaning out of her words. Wim looked up at her and actually blinked as if he didn't recognize her. *Then again,* Megan thought, *I was in jeans and a T-shirt this morning. Maybe he really doesn't recognize the vision of beauty I've become.*

"Oh, well, that's good," Dorfladen said, and actually turned away from them as if he had decided that the conversation was over.

Megan blinked and didn't say anything. Her father simply turned away as well, and the look on his face was worth seeing. It suggested, just for a flash, that he would have put Dorfladen over his knee and spanked him if he'd thought he could get away with it.

Halvarson was smooth about it. He just said, "And one more guest . . ." and led them off in another direction as if nothing had happened. When they were safely out of earshot, he said softly, "I'm sorry about that. It's a cultural thing, I think. I get this kind of treatment from that part of the world all the time, on the phone."

"I know," Megan's father said. Halvarson led them to an empty table not too far from the "swing band." He seated them, then said, "Do you want some real dinner instead of nibblies? Or would you prefer to do the buffet?"

"The buffet sounds good for me," Megan said.

"I'm with her," her father said.

"Then I'll leave you to it," Halvarson said. "I hope you'll excuse me . . . I have a few other matters to attend to."

They thanked him, and off he went across the room again, the consummate host.

Megan breathed out. "Kind of a mixed bag," she said to her father.

He nodded. "You're right there. Who was your friend?"

"Who? You mean Wim? He—"

"No, honey. The short gentleman."

"Oh! Daddy, are you kidding? Jacob Rigel?"

"The name's escaping me. Must be blood sugar."

"Must be. He runs High Black Enterprises."

Her father blinked at that. "Oh! The 'space jeep' guy."

Megan nodded. Rigel was famous in her book, and a lot of other people's. He had founded an industry producing small maneuverable spacecraft for industrial use, as well as for those private citizens who could afford them. There were rumors that his next-generation ships were going to be radically improved and vastly less expensive. Some people claimed that the business he was pursuing was going to change the world more radically than even the Net and widespread virtual access had. Megan wasn't sure about that, but it was certain that his invention, and his drive and determination, were going to open up "close space" in a way that all the governments now working in space hadn't been able to do. *I'm lucky to have met him,* she thought. *I'd really love to get a chance to talk to him for a while. . . .* But the thought made her strangely nervous. She didn't know what she'd say to someone like that . . . a pioneer, a genius.

"You're staring into space, honey. It's your blood sugar that needs attention, I'm thinking."

"Yeah. Let's do it."

They got up and carried out a thorough raid on the buffet. Megan had the caviar, and the lobster, and more of the caviar, with considerable emphasis on the sour cream, and there were salads *(I've got to try to be healthy about this. . . .)*, what appeared to be a cold roast beast, and a suckling pig that her father attacked with such ferocity that Megan started a series of vegetarian jokes that went on for the better part of the evening. There was also a peacock, or something masquerading as a peacock. Even Megan decided to go vegetarian at the prospect of having anything to do with that.

Around elevenish she noticed that her dad was starting to look tired. "Can you find your way back?" he said.

"No problem. Or they'll drive me."

"Great." He kissed her. "Have fun. I'll see you later. Don't worry about being locked out. The door knows our voices, apparently."

"Right."

He wandered off, said good night to Halvarson in passing, and headed out into the evening. Megan sat there wondering, for a moment, whether she was now going to have to deal with what's-his-name—Wim. She glanced over toward the table where the Dorfladens had been sitting, and was surprised to find them gone. *How do you miss someone that big leaving? It's not like he's fat or anything. It's just that he seems to take up more space than he's entitled to, somehow. . . .*

She shrugged and ate more of her last serving of caviar. More on her mind at this point than Dorfladen's size was whether anybody in the "front office" here knew who she really was and what she had come here for. *Maybe Halvarson?* she thought. *Nah, he thinks my dad is his spy.* This was not surprising considering that her dad had gotten a call from him within minutes of his talk with Winters. But he had betrayed nothing at all this evening in that regard, and anyway he was hardly likely to do so where any number of his staff could see. *Wenders, then?* Megan doubted it. Again there had not been the slightest flicker of recognition. . . . In fact Wenders had looked more annoyed at the sight of Megan than anything else. *Or maybe that means she does know. . . .*

There was no way to tell. Either way, there was nothing she could do about it now. In the morning she would start stirring around and seeing what she could discover. In the meantime, there was still the astonishing luxury of this place.

If I can't enjoy that, she thought, *there's something really the matter with me, no matter what else is going on.*

The last thing she did was have one more serving of the caviar and sneak a small glass of champagne—not that her father would have been annoyed with her, but drinking with him out of the way somehow had a cachet that drinking with him in the way didn't. She felt suddenly more adult than usual, sitting here all alone in a rich man's paradise, imbibing champagne and Beluga. . . . *This is the life.*

This is a life, some part of the back of her mind commented. *Like it? Don't get used to it. It's temporary.*

But the illusion of it not being temporary, of all this being her birthright, was pleasant. She finished that little glass of bubbly, brought her plate and glass back up to the buffet— "You didn't have to do that, Miss O'Malley!"—waved airily to the remaining guests, not noticing or caring whether they noticed her at all, and wandered out to the forecourt in front of the reception area.

The jitney in which they had come was sitting there. She climbed into the backseat and checked to be sure it was the same jitney driver who'd brought them. It was. "Home, Mihaul," she said with a grin, "and don't spare the horses."

He gave her a look. "Is this your native century, Miss O'Malley," he said, "or are you just visiting?"

Megan snickered.

"Home it is," he said, and drove her back to the villa. There the lights came on all up the drive at their approach, and the door opened for her at the sound of her voice. She waved to Mihaul, who had been waiting to see her safely in, and he left with a little showoff wheelspin that sprayed gravel.

Megan grinned and wandered up into her bedroom, the lights going off behind her and coming on before her. She sighed and flopped down on the bed, and reached for the Xanadu User's Guide to see if there was anything she might have missed. . . .

The sun was shining straight into her eyes. Megan opened them, looked around her in shock.

It was morning, and she was lying there still dressed from

last night, and her mouth tasted like the bottom of a fish farm.

Never, never, never eat caviar and then go to bed without brushing your teeth, Megan thought, rather distressed. She bounced up off the bed and hurried into the bathroom.

About an hour and a half later she came out again, as pink as her father had been the day before, having tried every sanitary device in that bathroom and having become very, very clean in the process. It took her only a few minutes to dig through the drawers and come up with a middie top and a pair of shorts and sandals—anything else would have been too hot. It already felt like it was about eighty degrees outside.

Megan went downstairs to the kitchen to rummage for something to eat and was extremely surprised to find a lobster in the refrigerator. There was not a scrap of shell on it, and it was perfect right down to the tips of its rosy pink claws. Next to it on the shelf of the refrigerator was a small sealed envelope with the stylized *X* motif of the resort in blue in one corner.

Megan picked up the envelope, opened it and took out the card inside. Written on it in a neat small spidery hand was:

I asked how they did it, and still don't understand the explanation. You'd better go see Milish Endervy in Catering. He sends you this with his regards. A.

"Daddy," Megan said loudly, "has anyone been in here this morning?"

No response. This place was nothing like home, where if you screamed loud enough, sooner or later the person you wanted would hear. This place was more like screaming in Grand Central Terminal.

She stood there and looked at the lobster. "Is it immoral to eat lobster for breakfast?" Megan wondered out loud.

"What?" her father said from behind her. He looked a little haggard.

"Are you okay?"

"I'm fine. I've just got a little heartburn. What's that?"

"Breakfast," Megan said, showing him the lobster and the note.

He regarded both. "They must have delivered that last night, before we came back. Meanwhile, breakfast? And you think kippers in the morning are strange?"

"Yes. Have you seen the mayonnaise?"

"There's some up in the cupboard."

Her father made himself a cup of tea and went away. Megan went rummaging for the mayonnaise and a lemon. "So when do you have to start?" she asked.

Her father sighed. "They want me to do an initial seminar later this morning."

"That's awfully soon. Aren't they going to give you a day to settle in?"

"Oh, it's no problem. You know what I'll be doing."

"The first-day doom-and-gloom riff," Megan said.

"Come on, it's not that gloomy. But, yes, that one. Then in the afternoon, if we have any takers for more serious work . . . well, we'll see."

"I'll go take the orientation tour, then," Megan said. She was not going to discuss exactly what she was looking for . . . since it had occurred to her more than once that anyone with the computer expertise to import her own workspace here without so much as a by-your-leave could possibly have arranged for the normal emergency/security monitoring devices installed in the villas to behave in abnormal ways. *In fact,* she thought, *I hope it was enough that I overwrote that data that Winters sent me. It wouldn't help to have whoever's behind the trouble here see that stuff in my files. . . .*

She sighed. She would have to look into that later. But right now she had more important things to contemplate. Megan sat down and ate the lobster from clawtips to tail without the slightest pang of conscience. Then she went down the hall to the utility room off the front door, where the bikes were kept, rolled one of them out, and walked it across the gravel of the front toward where the pavement started. The gravel, she noticed, had been raked since last night. *Boy, they take their service seriously here. . . .*

As she went, she thought she heard something from off to her left. Megan paused, looked in that direction. Someone was shouting, it sounded like: a big voice, deep, like a bull's. *And not a bull I'd care to meet at the moment,* Megan thought. Angry. Dorfladen, having a conference call with somebody, maybe? *If this is a sample of his management style, I'll pass.*

Fortunately he wasn't a problem she had to deal with. She got up on the bike and pedaled away through the sunshine and dappled shade in the direction of the main reception facility.

Had she not been at the party the night before, she would have had no way to tell that there had ever been one. Now the place simply looked like a large and understated hotel lobby, with one extremely long reception desk and one shorter one. As she came in, a couple of staff people in blue Xanadu uniforms—T-shirts, in this case, and lighter-colored shorts—came out to the desk to meet her. "Good morning, Miss O'Malley!"

I have a feeling that after two weeks of this, I'm going to prefer "Hey, you...." "Is there a general orientation tour of the control facility any time soon?" she asked.

"Ten minutes, if you'd like to wait for a few of your fellow guests. Otherwise one of us can take you through right now."

"Uh, no, I'll wait," Megan said, "thanks." She strolled out into what had been the party area last night, and which was now a lounge area with a table off to one side laden with fruit and other snacks.

Megan left this alone, finding that a whole lobster for breakfast had filled her up pretty conclusively. A few more guests came filtering in over the next few minutes—a couple of youngsters, a slim young man, and one of the people Megan had noted last night as not enjoying herself particularly, a tall well-dressed silver-haired woman whose face had too few lines for her age, and whose expression suggested that she might drink vinegar instead of coffee in the mornings. Megan joined them, greeted them casually, and one of the two Xanadu staff people, a slim blond young man whose name tag read MARK, waved them through the space between the counters and through the door in the paneling behind them.

The door gave onto a long hallway, and at the far end of the hallway was another wall, a glass-brick one with a door made of what looked to be the same electively opaque glass Megan had seen in the villa's downstairs bathroom. Mark spoke to it, and the door cleared and slid aside for him. "This way," he said, and led the little party through into Xanadu Operations.

Megan didn't say much during the tour, just concentrated on what they were being shown . . . which was, effectively, very little. As they walked around it on a raised walkway, Xanadu Ops looked to Megan much as any other big operational affairs center would have to these days. Lots of computers all over the place, virtual-access and physical-access, some clearly Net-connected and others clearly not, lots of big displays of various logistical systems around the island, everything from normal climatic control of the physical plant and other buildings to air-traffic control. Mark's talkover was interesting enough, but it told Megan little she didn't already know from the Xanadu User's Manual. When it was all over, and Mark had asked everyone else if there were any questions, and the other few guests started to drift away to be led off by another Xanadu employee, Megan said, "Uh, Mark—"

He nodded. "What can I do for you?"

She grinned. "Something a little more detailed, maybe. I talked to Len MacIlwain and Nasil Rajasthani last night. They said they would walk me through some of the techie stuff."

"Oh, sure, come on in."

He led her down a small flight of stairs into the great wilderness of computer monitors and virtual boxes and staging areas below the perimeter walkway. Down here on the "shop floor" she could see in more detail an animation being refined at one workstation, a piece of live holofootage being trimmed or augmented before it was incorporated into a scenario at another. It all seemed to be happening at considerable speed, but then it would have to, if these people were doing as many pavilions per year as the first guide had suggested. "Len?" Mark called. "Oh. Nasil, you see Len?"

A head popped up from around the speaker "wings" of a virtualia-auditing chair. "He went out for something to drink. Oh, hi, Megan. Bored with the real world already?"

She made a slight face. "My father claims I've been bored with it since birth."

"Then this is the place for you. Take a seat. Thanks, Mark. Hey, where is the snack stuff from Catering? It was due ten minutes ago."

"I think they're milking the cows for more cream or something." Mark grinned.

"Well, tell them to hurry up!"

Nasil sat back in his access chair again as Megan came around to look at what he was doing. He had a big "repeater" monitor in front of him, and on it some complex multicolored schematic was sketched out in three dimensions, but Megan hadn't the slightest idea what it involved. It could have been anything from a wiring diagram to a representation of a sewage system. "Thanks for taking time out for me," she said.

Nasil looked a lot more relaxed in a Xanadu T-shirt and chinos than he had in a tux last night. "No problem," he said. "It's business as usual around here today, at least so far. We have a couple of people taking initial delivery on pavilions this afternoon, but that's, oh, three whole hours from now. I refuse to think about any of that until the coffee guy arrives."

"You look awful relaxed about it."

"Why shouldn't I be? It's not like we build a pavilion in a day and never let the person who commissions it near it until we're done. That's a great way to have a client say it stinks and pitch a big fit and get you fired." He snickered. "These people have had a few quick 'fittings' before they come down here for their first full tryout. We fly them in and out like crazy. Why do you think we need our own air-traffic control? And frankly, the workload the guys in most towers stateside are under, we'd sooner handle it ourselves. If they dropped one of our clients into the water, there would be so many lawsuits on the horizon that you could walk back to the mainland on them."

Megan nodded at that, glancing around her. At that point Len came stepping down from the walkway with a cup of something steaming hot, looking if possible even more nerdy than he had the previous day. He, too, was in T-shirt and slacks, now, and he was wearing little round glasses like Nasil's. They looked oddly like brothers. "Couldn't stay away from the hardware, huh," he said.

Megan shook her head. "Not a chance. Look, I'm grateful you're even willing to let me be down here. But do you usually let people come wandering through, looking over your shoulders like this? I mean, everything here is proprietary, from the content to the delivery systems. Aren't you afraid you'll start having visits from industrial spies?"

"We get them all the time," Len said. "Mostly we treat them with the 'kill-them-with-kindness' routine. We drown them in data till they can't tell what's important or not."

"Besides, you're still not seeing anything that you'd be able to make much out of," said Nasil. "Behind anything that's happening out here in the open today, there are millions of lines of code. Billions, in some cases. We could even tell you how it's all done and you'd have trouble duplicating the most important processes."

"So tell me how it's done," Megan said.

Nasil and Len shot each other an amused look.

"This is the end of one of those old thriller vids, isn't it?" Len said, and grinned. "The bad guy has the good guy tied up and about to be eaten by crocodiles—"

"Or chopped up with lasers—"

"—and so he tells him all about his evil plans in detail."

Megan laughed. "Yeah, well, you can bring on the crocodiles at your leisure. Give me a break here! I haven't had a chance to read the press releases. But everyone seems to think you've found some kind of new back door into the brain, that much I know. Or some way to exploit some old one. Are you playing with midbrain stuff?"

Len raised his hands in what was only partly mock horror. "Might as well just stick knitting needles into people's heads."

"Kind of dangerous, that," said Nasil. "Any part of the brain that's still mysterious enough for you not to be sure which parts do what, or why, better to stay out of there."

"Hindbrain then?" Megan said.

"Warmer," Len said.

"But you wouldn't play with the autonomic parts of the brain, either," Megan said. "Not the cerebellum . . . that's just breathing and heartbeat and stuff. . . ."

"Getting hot," said Nasil. He and Len glanced at each other, enjoying this.

Megan made a wry face. The "performing smart kid" act occasionally had its uses, but with these two she was starting to wonder who the kids were. "That doesn't leave much to work on," she said, and started thinking about the "map of the brain" from her human anatomy unit in bio. She shook her head, unable to see what these two might be getting at.

"Limbic," said Len after a moment. "The limbic network."

Megan looked a little doubtful at that. "I thought that was mostly an old part of the brain that's used to handle smell."

"A lot more than just that, it turns out," said Len. "Everybody else feeds sensorial info into the brain via cranial nerves and so forth. Big fast nerve trunks, real easy to feed big bandwidth down. . . ."

"But there are limitations on that bandwidth," Megan said. "The body itself limits how much info can come down nerve trunks. You're saying access into the limbic areas is faster?"

"Not faster. But wider," said Nasil. "Those may be primitive parts of the brain, yeah. And it's true they don't handle much but smell and some other basic processing anymore. Because they're so old and basic, though, those parts of the brain lend virtual content a special quality."

" 'Special' how?"

The two of them gave each other sidelong looks. "Wait and see."

Megan had to laugh again. "Ooh, mysterious. Well, you guys must have made a lot of money by now, because now that you've dumped the company's secrets, I don't think you're going to have these jobs much longer!"

Now they laughed at her. "Yeah, well," said Nasil, "now all you have to do is go home and write fifty billion lines of code to implement the limbic access."

"Seventy," Len said.

"Pedant."

"Yeah, well at least I can count—"

"All right, all right!" Megan said. "I guess I should go see if this effect is so special."

" 'If'?"

"I think she doubts our sincerity."

They snorted in near perfect unison.

"So can I see one of the pavilions?"

"Sure," said Len. "We keep several 'sample' installations for browsing through. First Moon Landing, Kennedy Assassination, Crystal Palace Exposition, Escape from Pompeii . . ."

"That one sounds good," Megan said. Her father had said something about that simulation. She would save the Moon and the Crystal Palace for later—they were simulations she might want to linger over. An exploding volcano scenario— that was likely to be over fast, one way or another.

"Right," Len said. "Half a sec."

He picked up a small black rod from the nearby desk. "Where's your present implant?" Megan pointed at the right spot on her neck. "Oh, good, just a cricoid floater." He waved the rod at it, then chucked the rod back on the desk.

"That's it?" Megan said.

"That's it. Just a software solution. We tell the implant what areas you've got access to, and then instruct it in a slightly different routing to areas that are already mapped. . . ." He grinned then. "Well, enough of that, or someone will show up with crocodiles . . . and feed me to them. But when you're ready, just go straight down the main hall from the reception center"—he pointed off to the right, out the door of the office—"and tell them you want to use the Pompeii pavilion."

"That's all?"

"That's all. What, do you think we want to make this difficult for people? How are we going to get you to save up for the next ten years so that you can come down here again and get us to make up something special just for you?"

Megan nodded. "The first one's free, huh?"

"This is a business," Len said. "As they keep reminding us." He rolled his eyes. "Budgets. Bottom lines. If they'd give us some decent money, we could really do something.''

"But don't take our word for it,'' said Nasil. "Go see what we can do on a shoestring.'' Then his eyes widened a little. "You don't have any history of heart problems, do you?''

"Huh? No.''

"They're supposed to check before they let you onto the island, but I always ask. It never hurts to be sure. Okay. Have fun in Pompeii.'' He looked around him. "Where is the catering guy?''

"He was out in the hall, talking to Milish.''

"Why does that name sound familiar?'' Megan said.

"Huh? Milish? Milish Endervy. He's the head chef. Chief of Catering, I should say. Most head chef types are never supposed to come out of their kitchens, but no one seems to have told him that.''

"Milish . . . He sent me a lobster,'' Megan said suddenly.

"Typical. Watch out for him. He's a real smooth operator.''

Megan chuckled.

"Don't take our word for it,'' said Len. "Go see him yourself. Out the side door and look both ways. They're probably still out there.''

"Okay,'' Megan said. "Thanks, guys! Can I come back later?''

"Yeah, sure, tell us how it ends,'' Nasil said.

Megan waved to them and headed for the door. When she came out in the hallway, sure enough, there was a guy in Xanadu blues with a trolley bearing a coffee urn and an assortment of pastries, and another man, young and broad-shouldered and a bit thick around the waist, wearing a white double-breasted chef's coat, black-and-white checked pants, and a white hat rather like the close-fitting giant skullcap that some Asian tribes favor. Both of them looked curiously at her as she strolled down to them.

"They're getting crazy for sustenance in there,'' said Megan to the guy with the trolley. "Better get in there before they do something rash.''

"Caffeine fiends,'' the guy with the trolley said, and trundled it away.

The head chef looked at Megan and said, "So how was the lobster?"

"It was delicious. Thank you," Megan said, and held out her hand. He took it and shook it.

"You must have been pretty hungry when you got in last night," said Milish.

"No, I had it for breakfast."

He gave her an incredulous look. "That's enthusiasm."

"What I really wanted to know," Megan said, "was how you get the shell off without messing it up."

Milish nodded. "Step back here."

He led her farther down the hall, then to the right through an unadorned glass doorway. Suddenly they were standing in a sea of white tile and brushed stainless steel—an industrial kitchen, spotlessly clean and full of heavy-duty cooking equipment being tidied up. "This is the service kitchen for the evening events," he said. "We're not really that busy at this end at lunchtime. A lot of people prefer to go to the restaurants. Sometimes there aren't even enough people needing meals in their pavilions to warrant more than a few plates of sandwiches." He looked rueful. "I wish that happened reliably. At a quiet time like that I can take myself off to one of the more peaceful parts of my domain, like the herb garden or the dairy. Not this week, though. We're full up."

"The dairy?" Megan said. "Wait a minute! Nasil said something about milking the cows. I thought he was joking."

Milish nodded. "Some of the things that're hard to get absolutely fresh here are milk and cream," he said, "especially since we're three hundred miles from the mainland. We've got good transit, but we can't always control what happens before we get our hands on the product. And since we *are* out here on an island, I think the vendors assume we're too far away to notice if they pull a fast one. So we started a small dairy herd here, on the slopes of the mountain. All Jerseys—they don't mind having only a small pasture to graze. They were genetically engineered for just that, four hundred years ago." He looked at her and wiggled his eyebrows up and down. "Fresh milk every morning and evening, buckets of cream, not to mention yogurt and cottage cheese, and we make our own 'green' cheeses, as well.''

"Green cheese," Megan said, and grinned, suspecting she was having her leg pulled. "Like what the moon's made of."

Milish gave her a dry look. "I may not look like a techie type," he said, "but I do know what the moon's made of. Stop by the dairy later if you like. I'll show you the setup."

"I don't know if there's going to be time today," Megan said. "Tomorrow, maybe?"

"No problem. Meanwhile, about the lobsters . . . we grow them here as well—"

And he led her down to the end of the kitchen, where the aquaculture tanks were, and showed her how the dish was done. The process was not terribly gory, but it wasn't for the squeamish, either. It involved learning exactly where in a lobster to stick the knife, and not minding how the lobster wiggled around (its nervous system not yet having heard the news that its brain was dead), and then some careful work with an extremely strong and sharp pair of scissors. "The armor's still flexible before you cook it," Milish said. "It's only during cooking that the chemical reaction sets in that makes the shell brittle. All you have to do now is poach the lobster very gently in a court-bouillon, chill it, and serve it." He chucked the shears into a sink full of soapy water. "You want this one?"

"After eating one for breakfast? Perhaps not at the moment. Milish . . ."

"Oh, come on, a little more seafood won't hurt you. You can have it for dinner. Want some lime mayonnaise to go with it?"

"Uh, yes. Thanks," Megan said. "I really have to get going. . . ."

Milish smiled at her. "Don't forget about the cheese," he said, showing her to the door.

Megan was left with the better part of three-quarters of an hour to kill. She headed out front again to find her bike, starting to wonder about the logistics involved in running not just a normal luxury hotel, but a place like this, three hundred miles out in the middle of the ocean. *Serious costs*, she thought. *Billions of dollars.*

Who would benefit from knocking over an operation like this? Causing a high-end resort-cum-virtual-entertainment operation to crash?

She stopped in the act of wheeling her bike out of the shade where she had parked it, and paused to look up over her shoulder at Mount Xanadu, about which there were all those interesting rumors of hollowness.

Leave the entertainment out of it, she thought. *This would be a terrific piece of territory for someone to own.* Someone who didn't much like one of the major powers in North America . . . or didn't much like the powers in South or Central America, or Europe, either. The island was almost too well placed. These days three hundred miles was a walk in the park for some shoulder-launched weapons, let alone missiles. There were entirely too many forces and movements in the world who would find a piece of real estate like this the ideal place from which to stage an attack on an enemy . . . or from which to simply sit and attempt to enforce emotional blackmail on one or another of the neighbors.

Am I possibly just being paranoid about this? Megan thought. *Maybe it isn't geopolitical. Attacking the clients is likely enough to make someone really rich. Twenty million dollars from the poor guy in Miami. That sounds pretty good for starters.* For she could not believe that the person or persons responsible for that crime would stop there.

Something told her that their crook was angling for bigger results.

She rode off under the palms, mulling it over. It was time to enjoy the scenery and do some thinking until the hour was up.

Forty-seven minutes later she was back, walking down the long hallway in the computer center again. The secondary control area connected to that hallway had a much quieter, more restrained feel about it than the huge, open, sunny space where she had met Nasil and Len. The lighting was indirect, the carpeting was as thick as the stuff up in her bedroom, and the Xanadu staff lady sitting behind another counter, a lower one than those in the reception area, looked at her thoughtfully.

"Megan O'Malley?" she said.

"That's me."

"You're going to try the 'Escape from Pompeii' scenario?"

"Yes, please."

The staff lady glanced down at the console hidden behind the counter. "Let me check—yes, you have a parental authorization on file that covers any of our public simulations. Would you turn around for me, please? Thanks. That's fine. The scan shows the adjustments to your implants are completed. If you'd like to go in—it's the room right at the end of the hall, the last door facing you. Go in and make yourself comfortable, and when you're ready to begin, just say 'start.' When you've had enough, say 'stop.' I'm sure that you know what will happen. 'Escape from Pompeii' is a very intense experience, so if it gets to be too much, please keep in mind that it's easy to end the scenario."

Megan nodded and went down the hallway. The lighting here was even more subdued than out by the desk. The hallway was very anechoic, and the feeling the dimness and quiet produced was a little claustrophobic in comparison with the light and airiness of everywhere else Megan had been so far on the island.

The heavy wood-paneled door slid aside as she approached it. Soft lights came on. The room was shaped like a sphere with a flattened bottom. The walls of the sphere were covered with a layer of some deep blue sound-absorbing substance. In the center of the room was what seemed a very plain computer lineup chair, with no other hardware showing anywhere. There was something almost ominous about it, the plainness somehow suggesting that this was not going to be the usual virtual experience. Megan sat down in the chair and swallowed once, with a little difficulty. Her mouth was suddenly dry.

"Start," she said.

The world went dark, and she was overwhelmed by the smell of something burning.

When her eyes opened again, she was standing on a hill-side, in a lemon grove. There was something peculiar about the color of the sky, or rather the light coming from it: a leaden quality, like the light just before a heavy thunderstorm. She turned and looked around her. The trees hemmed her in on three sides, thick, their leaves drooping as if they had been starved for rain lately. The tart lemon-skin smell was all around. But so was that stench of burning. And down the hillside, where the trees opened out, Megan could see the cause of the smell.

Vesuvius. The mountain was belching out great clouds of black smoke and pale ash, and through the veiling cloud she could see, crawling sluggishly down the slope, the sullen glow of lava. *Not really crawling, though*, she thought. It was doing fifty miles an hour, and she counted herself very lucky not to be anywhere near it.

Under her, the ground rumbled and shook. Not a serious tremor, but it was enough to start Megan running downhill— the top of a hill was nowhere to be in an earthquake. *The whole thing might slide out from under me. It might fall on me, too*, Megan thought, *when I'm lower down—* But this hillside was making her nervous. There was some memory niggling at her, something particularly unsavory that had happened on a nearby hill—

Herculaneum, she thought, coming down out of the thyme-smelling brush of the hillside onto a road. It was a Roman road, not ruined but brand-new—close-set cobbles, very even, with a high curb, running straight left and right before her. Off to her left was a small town, and to her right, the road to a larger city, lined with tall pointed poplar trees on both sides. Pompeii—

She turned and ran that way, for she had a better chance of escaping from Pompeii. Almost no one had made it out of Herculaneum. Another of the ground tremors hit, and this was a bad one, not the rolling side-to-side shaking kind that she had experienced once or twice during a short visit to Los Angeles, but the sharp, nasty "transverse" kind that takes the ground right out from under you like kicking a table. Megan went down, the breath knocked out of her, and not ten feet from her she saw the perfect line of that straight Roman road torn across like a sheet of paper, the two sides of it simply pushing past one another to left and right, and the farther segment of the road pushing up over the nearer one, revealing its five layers of careful construction as it broke and shattered into many pieces.

The piece of ground she was lying on began to tilt. Megan scrambled to her feet, tried to find her balance, wobbled, and nearly fell once more as the earth beneath her rocked again. Behind her, that sound of tearing stone happened again, and Megan found her footing for real this time and ran.

She dodged around the broken road and then back down onto it again a few hundred yards along, where there was an unbroken stretch. The cloud from the mountain was beginning to stretch in her direction. Megan's lungs were burning, and she started to gasp as she ran, wondering *What's the matter with me? I should be able to run this far without*— But the burning smell had been there when she first appeared, and she swallowed, remembering that there had been a lot of gases involved with the eruption that were invisible. Sulfides, cyanophosphates—*poison gas by any other name,* she thought. *Am I running into it, or away from it . . . ?*

The cloud was reaching closer toward her. The world here was now divided into two distinct parts—the bright sunshiny Mediterranean world, with the hot blue line of the sea drawn against the blue horizon, the hills and mountainsides dotted with white villas, rich peoples' summer houses, here and there the splash of color from someone's garden, and the world under the cloud, shadowed, a gauze of gray and mauve drifting over everything, always fed and thickened by the billow of dark cloud pillaring out of the broken, enraged mountain.

Megan ran, reminding herself that this experience was virtual, but the sheer terror of it nonetheless came as a surprise to her, and she had to keep gulping with a throat that went dry and stayed that way, no matter how virtual all this was. Nothing to do with the atmosphere . . . just plain old fear. Yet at the same time some part of her mind kept insisting that all this around her, the hot sun, the hillside, even the black clouds billowing up from the mountain, were perfectly normal . . .

and, more, that it was normal to think about them in Latin. Normally Megan only thought about Latin in class or during homework, while fighting her ongoing battle with the language in the annoyed knowledge that it was one of the two spoken languages of science, and would be useful for her eventually, even if right now the declensions were a serious pain in the butt. But now it seemed more natural than English, almost reassuring, like a mother tongue lost and refound.

Megan probed at that sense of niggling familiarity in a gingerly fashion, wondering if it might be of use.

Unfortunately there did not seem to be anything directional about it. She was going to have to find the harbor on her own. Where the road into town went straight through, several other smaller city roads met it, and Megan paused, looking around, then turned leftward into the one that went most sharply downhill. This was a street with smaller, finer cobbles, and a gutter on one side to take the filth away. Up the street she ran, past the high walls of the houses, all their gates shut. She heard no sound from inside any of them. In this paling, bleak light, everything looked stark and strange. Not too far away she could hear screams.

The ground rolled under her. Megan gulped. She did not want to be trapped in a narrow street, under walls that no one in this time had the engineering to make earthquake-proof, when another of those sharp tremors hit. Out into the main square, head for the harbor—

The main square was full of people running in all directions, crying to each other in voices hoarse with fear, staggering under armfuls of their possessions, then throwing their possessions down and running in terror as the murk in the air became a steady fall of ash, coming down thick and soft as snow. It began to pile up in the street with astonishing speed, choking the gutters, making the footing at first gritty and then treacherous, for the stuff slid on itself and slipped under her feet. The screams got down inside her and made her guts seize with fear. She strangled a scream that started to work its way up outside her, took a breath, and actually had to hold it to keep another scream from coming out. People were plunging in all directions, staggering, falling, their own cries of terror muffled in the ash as they fell into it, bursting out again in fits of coughing and fitful shrieks as they tried to get up again, start breathing again, and sometimes couldn't. The panic was like a noose around Megan's own throat, constricting, holding her motionless and helpless. She tried to break herself out of it by force, to make herself go staggering step-by-step through the ash, trying simply to keep going downhill as the footing got worse and the visibility closed in to something like a thick fog. But as she fought the ash and the obstacles surrounding her, the worst obstacle was inside her—that nearly crippling sense of fear that made it impossible to act fast or think clearly. But she kept fighting.

Finally Megan had to make her way over toward one side of the street so that she could keep her hands on the walls of the buildings on that side as she headed downhill. Even with the wall's support, she tripped, picked herself up again, kept going. Her lungs were really burning, this time. *It's not healthy to breathe this ash,* she thought. *But it's really not good to stop and be buried in it, either. Or to be caught in a lava flow a few minutes later—* The terror nearly disabled her again.

She struggled on. Black flakes started coming down with the gray, and a few were not black but red. She was shocked to smell, then to feel, burning hair on her scalp. *This isn't supposed to happen!* she thought, with reason. Megan routinely kept her default "pain" settings turned right off during virtual experience, feeling strongly that life had enough genuine pain in it already to preclude the need for any "recreational" pain at all. *But this is Xanadu,* Megan thought, gulping. *"As real as the real thing."* Real enough for them to want to override your own preferences . . . sort of the way life does. She stopped and slapped desperately at her head, burning her hands as she beat out the smoldering ash that had briefly set her alight. Gasping, Megan staggered on, and inside her head someone began trying to pray to various gods whom Megan suspected were not able to do much about this situation. The only god who seemed to be on duty today was the one who the stories said lived in the volcano and forged thunderbolts there, and he was certainly working overtime.

The ash was piled up shin-high in the streets now, and it was heavier than it looked—she would have thought it should have been light and powdery, easy to kick aside, but the deeper it got, the more it asserted itself as having some relationship to stone. It was beginning to suck all the moisture out of the air, Megan suspected, and would shortly start setting like concrete. Her head ached and her lungs burned worse than ever, and it would have been so nice just to sit down in the overhang of one of these roofs and rest a little before going on. . . . But Megan knew perfectly well that if she ever did that, she would not get up again. She would wind up as one of those pitiful ash-defined shapes that the archaeologists had dug up years back—a boy curled up in fetal position near a street corner, a desperate dog, chained and still struggling to get loose even as it died, a man crouched down over his basket of bakery bread, hoping that the shower of ash would pass and trying to save the bread from being spoiled. . . .

Except that this is virtual, this is virtual. . . .

Keep telling yourself that, she thought.

She staggered on, feeling her way, building by building, tripping over things as she went. She knew what those things were. She would not look at them. Megan's eyes burned and stung and began to swell from the fine powdery ash getting into them. The terror and the hopelessness were closing in on her as thick as the ash in the air, as unavoidable. She would never get out of this. It was useless. Thousands of people had died in this cataclysm of the ancient world. What made her think that she would do any better—

Still, she kept going. It seemed to her that the downhill route was getting steeper, and then suddenly she missed her footing and fell. Hard stone edges hit her in the shoulder, the back, the upper right arm. She stopped, pushed herself up out of the ash, spat it out of her mouth, and tried to clear it out of her nose. Those were stairs she had fallen down—one of the broad stairways that led down to the docks. She pushed herself to her feet, tried to walk down them, and fell again. But as she did, she caught a glimpse of a lighter area in front of her than the gray, darkening haze through which she had been making her way, it seemed, forever. The air was getting clearer. She heard the sound of screams, cries, but very remote. Across the water . . . ?

She made her way toward the light. The vista before her began to pale, not the bleak bleached ash-light but something warmer, sun reflecting off water. A few more steps into the now intolerable brilliance. The sun came blooming through the falling ash as if through mist. For the first time Megan felt a breath of wind. *The wind, it's changing. . . .*

She staggered down into the clearer air where, bizarrely, the sun was shining. The screams were coming from the decks of the few boats still at the docks. People were swarming up ladders and ropes onto them. Megan ran as fast as she could to the closest one, saw a ladder leaned against its side, and went up it as quick as a rat, feeling just a flicker of humor as she caught sight of any number of rats swarming up the ropes, which still held the ship to the marble stanchions of the docks. Even as she made it up over the rail to fall gasping to the deck, someone not far from her grabbed the rope and tossed it overboard, where it and more desperate rats hit the water together. "Row!" someone yelled. "Row for your lives!"—and the ship began to stand away from the shore as the first flakes of ash began to fall on its deck. . . .

It was a long while before Megan felt well enough to do as the hundred or so other people aboard were doing: cling to the rail and look back at the doomed city. It was gone, completely hidden in a pale silvery cloud of death. Vesuvius continued to emit great curdled shapes of black and gray cloud, and the orange streams of lava wound sluggishly down the mountain's side. From the ship came the sounds of weeping. Megan wept, too, though it stung her lacerated eyes. A whole city, wiped out between breakfast and lunch. "Why did they do it?" she whispered.

A man next to her looked at her strangely. "Who? The gods?"

"No, I mean the people who lived here. They knew the mountain was active. Why did they stay here?"

The man shook his head and shrugged. "Nice climate," he said.

Megan thought of her visit to Los Angeles and produced a slightly twisted smile. "Stop," she said.

—And she was in the chair, in the somber, spherical room, and everything was silent.

Megan got up and brushed herself off.

Then she laughed, but it was not a laugh of pleasure. *All the time I was trying to remember that this wasn't real, the reality of it kept distracting me,* she thought. *I was terrified. And no matter how many times I reminded myself, I kept losing track of the fact that none of it was real. Since when have I ever reacted like this to something virtual? . . . They're really on to something here.*

She went out of the room, back down the hall, and paused by the desk. The Xanadu staffer there looked at her.

"How are you?" she said.

"Amazed," Megan said.

"Any ill effects?" the lady said.

Megan shook her head. "Thanks," she said, and headed out the way she had come. She took it slowly, partly because the world looked strange to her at the moment—no falling ash, no sounds of screams—and partly because she was thinking about some of the more uncomfortable aspects of what she'd just experienced.

No wonder, she thought. *No wonder people pay so much for this.* It was not just the virtual experience; that would have been available elsewhere, anywhere good programmers had been at work on the Net. But this—it was not just like experiencing something, it was like "feeling" it for the first time as well: feeling emotions themselves as if they were something fresh and new, as if they were fed down a new set of nerves . . . *if only for an hour, an evening, a day. That's the attraction,* she thought. *Imagine that you had some really seriously stressful job, one that had made you tired of the normal grind of life, and all you wanted was—not just to forget your troubles but to remember what feeling, say, pleasure felt like when fed down "a new set of nerves." Come here, pay the price—and genuinely feel things, as if everything was new. For a while.*

That could be worth a lot. More than a lot . . .

Coming out of the interior hallway into the reception center, Megan looked around with some surprise to see that it had been converted again and was now serving a buffet lunch. She found, though, that she had no appetite. All the food looked strange to her somehow—excessive, inappropriate—after having seen the deaths of so many people. *Later,* she thought. *Maybe.*

She got out into the bright sunshine and found her bike. Megan considered going straight to her father's seminar, to see how it was going. He should be starting right about now. *But, no,* she thought then. *I want a shower.* Another unusual symptom. She could never remember having felt so physically affected by a virtual experience—not when she was back in the real world. She was itching all over, like someone who had recently fallen down repeatedly in pumice ash.

She mused over this as she rode away from the reception center. The limbic part of the brain, they had said. A very ancient part. Smells were indeed one of the things it still handled—and she recalled how very vivid the smells had been in the experience, how they had been almost the first thing she noticed. But elementary emotions—fear, joy, anger—were supposed to be "located" there, too. The Xanadu software and hardware were doing something to this area, or through this area, that no one else had managed. Something rather scary . . .

Suddenly she felt as if she could use a little reassurance. She turned down the side lane that led to the "function center," where her dad's seminar would be taking place, a small building rather in the same style as their villa. Megan left the bike in the shade of a tree, went inside. In the front hallway was a liquid-crystal sign listing various events happening there today. One of them read O'MALLEY, WRITING AS A HOBBY / WRITING AS A WAY OF LIFE, WING B.

She followed the discreet signs for Wing B and found a large room that looked like a cross between a university lecture hall and a living room conversation pit. There were desks stacked up in four circles of ten in each row, with comfortable chairs behind them. At the center/bottom of the room was another large desk, and another comfortable chair, and her father, with some notes scattered around him.

"Am I late or something?" Megan said, going down to him.

"No, early," he said. "They rescheduled me. I conflicted with lunch. Today is the Conch Festival, apparently."

Megan rolled her eyes. "I bet I know whose idea that is," she said.

"Oh, really. Where were you?"

"Pompeii," she said.

He looked at her with slight concern. "Did that one, did you?" he said. "Are you okay?"

The full version of the answer would have taken her a long time. For the moment she just nodded. "I want a shower, though. I thought I would stop in here first and make sure you were doing all right."

He smiled slightly. "No problems yet. Except with my own fragile ego, as you see."

She snickered. Her dad's ego, whatever else it might be, was not fragile. "You take that critic's influence too seriously," she said. "I know he said he knew how that last book was going to end within twenty pages. He was lying. Crabby old—"

"Please," her father said. Nonetheless, his smile was broader. "Loyalty," he said, "even when it may not strictly be deserved, is a noble thing. And it makes you want to deserve it." He kissed her on the top of her head, a gesture she usually ducked, but that today provided a sense of reassurance she was grateful for.

Megan retaliated in the only way available to her, by rubbing his bald spot. "I'll see you later," she said, and headed out the way she had come.

She rode back to the villa, parked the bike in the front, and paused for a moment. The soft hiss of the waves was audible through the trees. *Since when could I resist that?* Megan thought, and took the path around the side of the house, toward the beach. She paused briefly by the pool to watch some small tropical bird dive-bombing the surface of it again and again. At first she thought it was snapping up bugs from the surface of the water, but then she realized that there were no bugs. It was drinking, diving down time after time to take tiny sips from the surface of the pool.

I ought to put out some water for it, she thought, and wandered down the path toward the beach again. The soft hiss of the local surf slipping up the beach, then down again, washed other sounds out, even the screams in her mind.

She wandered out onto the coral sand, shaking her head at the way the Pompeii experience had affected her. *Limbic . . .* she thought. There was some memory about that word, something useful, that was eluding her.

Megan sighed and walked along the beach for a while, waiting to see if the memory would come back. It refused. She was left wondering what was going on at home, what her brothers were doing. Tearing the house up, probably. And then there was the question of her mother. *I wonder where Mom is at the moment*, Megan thought. *She would like this place.* She always complained that her life didn't have enough silences in it. This long, slow hissing, the white sun blinding on everything, the blue water, would appeal to her. A nice empty beach . . .

A near-empty beach, Megan corrected herself as she turned a curve and saw someone about half a mile away walking toward her. No, now he was walking away again. He hadn't seen her.

She knew, at a guess, who it was. *Well,* she thought, *do I feel like turning around and walking away, like a coward? Or do I feel like keeping the way I've been going, and meeting him, and knocking him down again?*

Her mouth tightened. *Let him take his chances*, she thought. She had seen, or rather felt, about a hundred thousand people die today. One spoiled brat more or less wasn't going to make her day any better or worse.

She just kept on walking. In about ten minutes she caught up with him.

He had never noticed her, this whole time. Wim was stalking back and forth like some kind of caged animal. As Megan wandered toward him, he looked up suddenly, saw her, and stopped, and stood very still.

Megan looked at him and wondered again whether he had told anyone—his father, for example—about their little encounter the night before. It seemed unlikely, though. From experience with her brothers, Megan had noticed that boys did not normally discuss details of who had recently knocked them over, especially if the person responsible was female.

She couldn't think what to do except walk on up to him as if nothing were the matter, then pause to look out at the water. "So, Wim," she said, "how're things?"

He stared at her. "You don't know?"

His vehemence surprised her a little, partially because it wasn't directed at her, and partially because he apparently genuinely expected her to know. "Uh, no, sorry, I've been out all day."

He stared out at the water. "Somebody destroyed one of my dad's companies last night," he said. "One of the big ones. It was being floated on the Hong Kong stock exchange, and somehow they drove the stock price down to almost nothing. All his other companies have been hurt, too. I don't know exactly how they did it. All his people are running around going crazy trying to figure out what happened, but they don't understand it." Wim stood there with his fists clenched. "If I knew who to do it to," he said, "I'd hunt them down and scrooge them."

His sheer furious intensity was astonishing. Megan looked at him and suddenly thought of her father. Loyalty, he had said . . . a noble virtue. She found herself looking at Wim with something besides pity or annoyance. And at the same time an idea occurred to her.

"Look," she said. "I didn't have lunch. This isn't doing you any good. Come on and let's get a sandwich or something. You can tell me what happened . . . and we can think of something to do."

"Like what?" Wim said, with a brief access of the old scorn.

Megan gave him a meaningful look. "Revenge?" she said.

Wim looked at her thoughtfully, and then broke into a slow

grin that would have done credit to a great white shark.

"What kind of sandwich?" he said.

Megan grinned, too, and together they went back up toward the villas.

4

About fifteen minutes later they reached the main road, and not five seconds later Mihaul the driver in his little jitney came buzzing around the nearest curve and stopped for them.

"Drop you somewhere?" he said, waggling his eyebrows a bit.

"Lunch," Megan replied in kind, "and step on it."

Mihaul stepped, so fast that Wim had to clutch at the railing of the seat in front of him. "So what kind of lunch?" he said. "We've got the Conch Festival today—"

"I don't eat fish," Wim said.

Megan raised her eyebrows. A Caribbean island didn't strike her as the perfect vacation spot for a non-fish eater, though it was unlikely Wim had been consulted when his father picked the destination. "I seem to remember you mentioning a deli," she said.

"The Deli," said Mihaul. "Just what you're after. Or so I would guess. Big sandwiches?"

"Yes, please," Megan said.

Wim nodded. About five minutes of tropical scenery later they were in front of something extremely nontropical. It looked like a New York brownstone, one with a large delicatessen of the sit-down kind in the bottom story. Megan hopped out and said to Mihaul, "You mentioned pastrami the other night?"

"Pastrami-smoked salmon," Mihaul said, "but they do the other kind, too. Check it out."

Megan nodded as she hopped out. Mihaul sped away. Wim headed for the door, but she briefly caught him by the arm, pretending briefly to look at the menu posted in the window. "Have you ever noticed," Megan said softly, "that one of those little buggies always comes along nearly as soon as you get out on the road?"

"Service," Wim said. "We're paying enough for it."

"Yeah, maybe. So tell me—where are the cameras?"

He didn't say anything to that, but gave her a thoughtful look.

"Maybe we want to be just a little bit careful about what we say in there," she said. "Save the really juicy stuff for the beach. Or the bathrooms."

Wim gave her a look. "If you think I'm going in some bathroom with you—"

Megan rolled her eyes. "That's one of the places they definitely don't monitor in the villas, so it's that or the beach," she said. "And even the beach . . ." She stopped herself, wondering who might possibly even be listening to them now. "What kind of music do you like?"

"I don't like music."

Just what I needed, she thought. *Another reason not to like him.* "I've got a nice radio," she said. "We can go out to the beach and listen to it later. After lunch we can go back the way we came, and we can pick it up."

Wim looked at her oddly, then nodded. Together they went into The Deli.

A few moments later Megan began to see what Mihaul had meant when he called it "The" Deli. The place was done in archetypal last-century Formica, most of it apparently genuine, not cloned. The sandwiches and salad plates on the menu stuck in a wooden block on their table had tacky movie-star names, and the menu itself was a piece of laminated plastic that had apparently seen better days.

"This place looks kind of old," Wim said.

Megan raised her eyebrows. Apparently the delights of pur-
poseful retro-architecture were lost on Wim. "Never mind,"
she said. "I think the food is going to be just fine."

A waitress appeared, wearing a pink-striped uniform with
a white apron. "What can I get you kids?"

"Pastrami sandwich on wheat," Megan said. "Large."

The waitress regarded her amiably. "Is there any other
kind? Anything to drink?"

Megan scanned down the menu. "Cel-Ray tonic?" she
said. "What in the world's that?"

"Do you want me to tell you," said the waitress, "or just
bring you some and let you find out?"

"Tell me," said Megan.

"No, just bring me some first," said Wim. "Then tell
her."

Megan looked at him in surprise. *Damned if I'm going to
let him outdo me at something like this!* "Bring me one, too,"
she said, "and don't tell either of us."

The waitress smiled. "Sandwich for you?" she said to
Wim.

"Pastrami on rye. Large."

The waitress nodded and went off. Megan and Wim glared
at one another amiably for a few moments.

"I can't believe you didn't know what happened," Wim
said. "I thought everybody heard—around here, anyway.
Didn't you hear the noise?"

"Uh, yeah," Megan said. She was not going to add that
she had thought it was probably normal. "Look, Wim, just
tell me what happened to your dad."

That took some doing, at first, since Wim started the story
off with details about some trip to Switzerland that then had
to be aborted for a trip to Australia in his father's private
hopper, and then they had to go to New York to do some
shopping before they could see the accountants in Liechten-
stein. . . . On and on it went, and Megan could see less and
less what it had to do with anything except impressing her.
When he mentioned the polo ponies, she couldn't stand it
anymore. Megan put one hand over her eyes and said, "Wim,
look, would you do me a favor? I'm what you would probably

consider a poor person, normally, and this is getting really boring. I know you have all the money on earth, but I'd appreciate not hearing about it every five seconds.''

He looked genuinely shocked. ''I don't mention money every five seconds.''

''Yes, you do. In terms of what it can buy. All the stuff you take for granted that people like me couldn't have except as a special thing. Trips and clothes and polo ponies and private hoppers and limousines and all the rest of the stuff. It makes you sound like you're bragging all the time. And I know you're not bragging, I know you're used to all this stuff, but it gets so old. Give it a rest.''

''You're just jealous!''

''You're just dim,'' Megan said in complete scorn. ''Other people have nice lives without thousand-digit bank balances. If that's a problem, well, deal with it. There are six billion of us, and we have you outnumbered. Now are you going to tell me how they robbed your dad, for pity's sake?''

They glared at each other, but then had to cover it over somewhat as the waitress in the pink uniform suddenly appeared with two tall glasses full of ice and a nearly clear liquid that bubbled.

''Two Cel-Rays,'' she said, and put them down. ''You just give me the high sign when you both want to know exactly what it is you're drinking. Sandwiches'll be ready in a moment.''

She went off, and Megan and Wim both looked doubtfully at the glasses, then at each other. *I'm not going to wait for him*, Megan thought, and reached out for hers. Wim did so at the same moment—and they looked at each other.

Megan let just a small crack of a smile show. ''Bottoms up,'' she said, and lifted the glass, and smelled it.

A strange, aromatic scent. She put her eyebrows up and took a drink at almost exactly the same time Wim did. Then her eyes widened.

''Ewwwwwwwww!'' they said in perfect unison.

Megan had to crack up, then, as she put the glass down. ''What is that?''

''Not something I'm going to drink twice,'' Wim said. He

pushed the glass away, looking at it suspiciously. "When she comes back, I'm getting something normal."

"Make it two," Megan said. "So look . . . I'm sorry. Let's cut each other some slack or nothing's going to get done. What exactly happened to your dad?"

"Not to him," Wim said. "Or, not really. 'He' turned up at a director's meeting and told his directors to start the process of cutting one of his companies loose. Said he wasn't satisfied with its earnings over the past couple of years, and he wanted to cut his losses. So they got busy and did it." Wim looked rather satisfied through his sourness. "They don't sit around when he tells them to do things. The stock markets got wind of it. They took it as a sign of weakness in the company. All the conglomerates' stocks took a plunge."

Wim actually put his face down in his hands for a moment. "That was Thursday. But Thursday my dad didn't go to any meetings. We were on our way here. He was getting ready to take delivery on his new pavilion."

Megan nodded slowly. "Who would have known you were coming?" she asked.

Wim shrugged. "About fifty people. And everyone here."

"Right," Megan said. "But wait a minute. Everyone?"

"Look, are you blind? Everyone here knows us by name."

"They do now," Megan said. "But who would have known where your dad would be, and when? Who was he talking to at the company?"

Wim thought about that. "Halvarson. A couple of the guys in Tech who were supervising the actual construction of the pavilion. The travel people."

"Which guys?" Megan said.

"Uh, I'm not sure . . . I'd have to check. But my father was hearing from them a lot for the month before we came down here. He had to come in for a couple of fittings first."

" 'Fittings'?"

"Yeah, that's how they make sure the pavilion is going the way you like it. We came in from Zurich once, in the middle of a shopping trip . . . another time from Stockholm. Virtual checks aren't enough. You have to come physically. They won't let anything out of this place."

"It would help if you knew the names of the tech guys," Megan said.

Wim shrugged. "I can find out. But why are you so interested? Why should you care?"

She gave him a look at the sound of the old hostility in his voice. "Maybe I'm just bored," she said. "Or maybe things like this really get me cranked off. I don't know your dad from a hole in the ground, but maybe he didn't deserve having something like this happen to him, and maybe the idea that it did happen just annoys me."

Wim was still looking shocked at the idea that someone might not know his dad from a hole in the ground.

The waitress in the pink uniform arrived with a tray and two large plates completely occupied by towering sandwiches, that she put down in front of them. She also brought large, icy glasses of some kind of tropical cooler. "In case," she said. "Enjoy. Call me if you need anything."

She walked off leaving Megan staring in astonishment. Wim's sandwich alone appeared to have required about half a cow's worth of pastrami. "You'll never finish that!"

"Yes, I will," said Wim. "I have better things to do than obsess about my weight."

She gave him a look. "I do not obsess."

"You do. You should have seen yourself at the buffet the other night. Picky, picky, think about it for five minutes before taking another spoonful . . ."

Megan sniffed, thinking about pointing out that, whatever she did, at least she didn't stuff food into her mouth while talking. She let that pass for a moment and ate the pickle first, that being her favorite part, then began attacking the sandwich in a workmanlike manner, beginning by eating the parts that hung out the farthest. Her oldest brother had instructed her in this art a long time ago, explaining that pastrami, like spaghetti and a hot dog with the right amount of sauerkraut, was a sport food. "You get it," he said, "or it gets you. Don't get got."

Megan got busy getting it first. Across from her, Wim was engaged in a similar battle, but he seemed to prefer the strictly tactical approach to the strategic. As a result, for the moment, the sandwich seemed to be winning.

"So," Megan said after a few moments of work on her own sandwich. "What brought your dad down here in the first place?"

"Vacation," Wim said.

Megan shook her head. "I can't imagine him taking one."

Wim gave her a look over the rye bread. After a moment he put the sandwich down. "It's that obvious, is it?" he said, sounding glum. "Well, the vacation was kind of my idea."

This time she couldn't restrain her laughter. Wim glared at her.

"No, no," Megan said, putting the sandwich down, "I don't mean anything by that. I mean, this was sort of my idea for my dad, too."

"Where's your mom? Are they divorced?"

"Oh, God, no. She's off working. She's a journalist; she keeps getting dragged weird places with no notice."

"It sounds like fun," Wim said.

"It's not. Half the time the way we find out if there's going to be a war or a coup somewhere is that they send my mother to an out-of-the-way place for no apparent reason. The other half of the time she's at home embarrassing politicians or warning people that if they don't stop messing up, the world's going to end. She likes it, but I think she works too hard."

"My dad, too," said Wim. "He has to be flying all over the place, all of the time, overseeing this company, selling that one, buying another one somewhere else. I thought maybe getting him out in the middle of nowhere for a couple of weeks might let him slow down a little. But no such luck. He's brought all the work with him."

"My dad, too," Megan said.

They ate their sandwiches in glum unison for a few minutes more. "So he must have gone for the idea, anyway, since you're here," Megan said. "What kind of pavilion are they doing for him?"

"This time it's some kind of Roman orgy."

Megan stared. Wim cracked up. "Really," he said. "No, not that really. He tells me there's not actually sex in it or anything. It's a 'Bacchanalia.' It was in some opera he likes.''

"Which one?" said Megan. She was something of a classical music fan.

"It's Wagner. Uh . . ." He tried to remember. "Tannhaser."

No sex? Megan thought. *In that "Bacchanalia"? Boy, has this kid ever been shown an edited version.*

"Tannhäuser," Megan said. "Have they given you access to it?"

"Parts of it," Wim said. "Parts are private for my dad."

"Can we sneak in?"

Wim thought about that. "Have you got implants?"

"The general ones, yeah."

"I don't know if they'll work. All the implants for the custom pavilions have individual embedded passwords or something."

"Hmm," she said, and nodded. "Okay . . . This is something else for the beach, I think."

Wim nodded and went back to the systematic deconstruction of his sandwich. Megan did the same.

It took them about another half an hour to finish up and decline dessert. Megan, though, did something that astonished her. She drank the rest of the peculiar tonic as well as the fruit drink, and Wim, possibly not to be outclassed, did the same. When the waitress finally came to clear their plates away, she looked at the empty glasses and raised her eyebrows. "Grows on you, doesn't it?"

"What is it?" Wim said.

" 'Cel-Ray.' Celery tonic."

That was the weird flavor. It was astonishing, though, how well it went with the sandwiches. The two of them got up, shaking their heads, and Megan said, "I think I'll even have another one next time. . . ."

"I'll make a note of it," said the waitress. "Enjoy the day. . . ."

They wandered out into the tropical sunlight again. Sure enough, no sooner had they made it out to the main road than Mihaul came zipping along again. "Need a ride?"

"Not this time," Megan said immediately. "We'll walk."

He waved and headed off. The two of them made their way

back to the lane that served their villas, and then down by
the path around the back of Megan's villa.

"Wait half a sec," Megan said, and dashed into the villa.
Her father was nowhere to be seen, which for the moment
suited her fine. She found the "boom box," turned it on low,
making sure that the "graphic equalizer" was already engaged, and walked out with it again, meeting Wim around
the side of the house.

They headed down to the beach, with the boom box playing
some noisy third-stream jazz, which was having something
of a renaissance at the moment. Wim winced a little at the
sound of it, but didn't say anything for the time being, and
they made their way down to just above the tideline and sat
down on the coral sand.

"Okay," Megan said. "Look . . . about your dad. There's
no way we can go around trying to figure out who did it by
just asking people. If someone here is slick enough to do this
kind of virtual raid, they're slick enough to look innocent
while they deny everything and cover their tracks." She
sighed. "There's got to be a way to get into the Xanadu
systems and snoop around."

Wim looked skeptical at that. "Gonna be a good trick if
you can manage it," he said. "They've only got the most
tightly guarded proprietary system in the world."

"So they say," Megan said, and gave Wim a look. She
was thinking that publicity could be a wonderful thing . . .
and also that every system had a back door, no matter how
tightly the front one might be locked.

She was also wondering exactly how far into her confi-
dence to take him on this. She certainly wasn't going to mention Net Force at this stage of things. . . . *So what do I tell
him? That I'm a freelance criminal investigator? Megan
O'Malley, Private Eye? Fat chance . . .*

"Access to their system is the problem," Megan said. "I'm
sure it's implant-based, the same as for the pavilions. There
has to be a way to reprogram them for wider access. Maybe
some way to jimmy one of those 'magic wands' they use."
She sighed. "I want to check into this a little more. But after

I've had a chance to look into a couple of things . . . Can you get away this evening?''

Wim thought about that. ''It shouldn't be a problem,'' he said. ''Everybody is so upset, they're all running around like chickens without heads. No one's going to notice if I miss dinner.''

''Good. Come over to our villa, then. We'll get into their local Net and 'play around' a little bit . . . in an innocent kind of way. Better to have company.''

He looked at her strangely. ''How does two of us make it more innocent than one?''

''Because''—she didn't quite say ''you dimwit''—''if they see two of us hanging out together all of a sudden, they'll assume it's adolescent lust or something similar. One of us alone poking around the edges of their system would look suspicious. But the tropics are supposed to make everybody a little crazy. Let's use it as protective coloration.''

''Oh,'' Wim said. ''Okay.'' He said it with such unconcern that Megan realized, with great relief, that the merest idea of adolescent lust with her had never crossed his mind. With anyone else, Megan would have paused to wonder whether she should be insulted. But not in Wim's case. He clearly never thought about that sort of thing at all.

''Great,'' she said. ''Let's meet back here, then. Around nine tonight? It should be dark enough.''

''Okay.'' And he nodded and simply took himself off without bothering to say goodbye. Megan found herself wondering whether this was something that ran in Wim's family or something cultural. *Not my problem to deal with, thank heavens. Once we get this little difficulty cleared up, we're out of here.*

And not a moment too soon. Polo ponies!

She picked up the boom box and went up to the villa to freshen up, and this time, rather to her surprise, did run into her father. ''What're you doing here? What happened to your seminar?''

''They rescheduled me for tomorrow,'' her father said, puttering around the kitchen. ''Half a day wasted. Some of the people here don't know their own minds. The clients, I mean. The Xanadu people were very apologetic about it, but . . ." He shrugged. "Oh, and a delivery came for you."

"For me? What?"

He reached into the refrigerator and handed her a plate. On it was a small round white cheese, and next to it was a note:

Stop by and I'll show you how we make these.

Milish

"Is this guy some kind of secret admirer?"

"I doubt it," Megan said. "Just a foodie. He appreciates my appetite." She chuckled and put the cheese back in the refrigerator. "I'll have it for dinner, maybe."

"You're not going to have another lobster?"

She waved at him, not answering, and headed back out the French doors to take the path down to the beach. *The problem,* Megan thought, *with having as much lobster as you want, any time you want, is that suddenly it loses its rarity value.* And that was kind of sad. She might never look at lobster the same way again.

I wonder if this is the reason for some of those sad faces, she thought, coming out on the beach and walking in the opposite direction from the villas, off to the left, westward. *If you can have anything you want, any time you want, there's nothing that's special anymore. Maybe this is why some of these people start coming to Xanadu. The exclusivity of the place, just the fact that it's incredibly expensive and difficult to get into, itself becomes the whole point of the exercise. The experiences, maybe, become a side issue. . . .*

The thought made her feel even sadder. She sighed, pushed it aside, and took her shoes off to go down and walk in the surf. It was a long walk. She was curious to see how far the beach stretched, and she needed to get her thoughts in order. It was all very well to talk about breaking into anyone's computer systems, let alone Xanadu's. She needed to have a clear sense of what she was looking for, though, in case she did manage to get in. And the details of exactly how she would get in were still a little beyond her. *I think I might need to talk to Mark Gridley on this one*, Megan thought. *When I get back I'll pull out "Dad's laptop" and see what I can arrange. . . .*

She had walked nearly three miles, considering plans and rejecting them, considering new plans and rejecting those, too, by the time she spotted a lone figure in a black-and-orange-striped wet suit coming up out of the water, about half a mile farther on. The straightness of this particular beach kinked a little there. Two long spurs of black stone came out and formed a little sheltered bay, and at the tip of one of the spurs was what looked like a little beach shelter or cabana.

Why would anyone need a wet suit in water this warm? Megan wondered. She had been walking barefoot in it for a good while now, pausing every now and then to watch little fish that she had only previously seen in tropical fish tanks come sliding up with each wave to pick interestedly at the sand where her last footstep had been. Curious, she went to see what was going on.

To her surprise, standing there by a pile of assorted equipment was Jacob Rigel, his hair (what there was of it) very much askew because he had just taken off a snorkel and mask. He had a can of something in his hand. On closer inspection, Megan saw with some amazement that it was a familiar brand of cheese spread.

She burst out laughing. "Mr. Rigel—hi—but what's that for?!"

"Call me Jake, please," he said. "You'll make me feel middle-aged." He looked at the can. "The fish like it."

"You're kidding me."

He shook his head, dropped the can on the sand next to a waterproof plastic notepad, and sat down, starting to pull off his swim fins. "I haven't made up my mind about why they like it. Maybe they have no taste," he said. "Or, alternately, maybe they like things with strong flavors and smells. If you want to attract a lot of friendly tropical fish in a hurry, this is a great way to do it. Spray some in the water—suddenly you have hundreds of friends."

Megan sat down, too, fascinated. "Taking some time off?"

"From my life, yes," Rigel said, and sighed, and stretched. "Well, from the work part of my life, yes. Oh, you mean from something else going on here? No. This is what I came for."

"Snorkeling? You could do that somewhere less, uh—"

"Expensive? Naturally. But only some of this"—he pointed out at the water—"is real."

"The water?" Megan said, rather bemused.

"Well, yes. See—" Rigel pointed out into the little bay. "You can see the string of buoys out there, to keep people on sailcraft away. It's as much for their own protection as mine. The lagoon's been partially holomodeled for me as a very special coral reef, and custom stocked—there's wildlife here that wouldn't normally be found in this hemisphere. And up there"—he pointed at the "cabana"—"is an extension of the lagoon, into another reef they've built for me, a more virtual one. It's my pavilion." He smiled, looking out at the bay.

Megan blinked at that. "I thought all the pavilions were inside the main facility."

"Oh, no. Well, not mine, anyway. As for the other pavilions, they wouldn't have 'room' for all the people who would be in there experiencing them, and there are always people who want complete privacy, anyway. So they usually install access from the villas as well. People can dip in at full bandwidth without leaving them." He shook his head. "Seems a little boring to me. But what they've built me here—" He looked out over the water. "From up there in my pavilion, I can swim out there and go virtual, and suddenly you're above reefs or in underwater locales thousands of miles away. Some of them are real."

Rigel leaned back on one elbow. "I should explain," he said, "that I study coral. A lot of the coral I'm interested in, like the beds off the Great Barrier Reefs, is so protected that no one's allowed to swim there anymore, while the reefs regenerate themselves from all the damage done during the last century. I can't go there—but I can swim those reefs out here." He waved his hand at the bay. "I can swim over reefs that haven't existed for a thousand years . . . or a million.

They've re-created an Ordovician reef for me. I saw my first trilobite this morning.'' He grinned, and looked like a little kid at Christmas. "That's why the wet suit, really. I'd just as soon stay in the water all day without it, but if you stay in as long as I'd like to without any protection, you come out looking like a prune. Which I do anyway. And I have to watch my hydration. Which reminds me.'' He started rummaging among the various equipment in the pile and came up with a couple of water bottles, offered one to Megan.

"Thanks,'' she said, and had a swig. Rigel drained his.

"I knew some of the pavilions were pretty elaborate,'' Megan said, rubbing her arms. The offshore breeze was beginning to pick up a little, and it was slightly chilly. "But this is something else.''

Rigel smiled a small dry smile. "So was the bill.'' He looked out across the water.

"I should feel guilty,'' he said after a moment. "Third World countries could thrive for a month on what I'm paying for this week. Yet at the same time I need to rest from the work I do sometimes, so I can do that work better . . . and the stuff I'm up to may eventually make the difference between some of those Third World countries becoming Second World, or First World, or their not becoming much of anything at all.'' He looked at Megan again. "You know what I'm working on?'' he said.

"A little. The 'space jeep.' ''

He nodded. "It seemed like such a simple thing,'' he said. "I couldn't believe that no one else had run with the idea before I came along and picked it up. . . . But think about this. Look at the world's equatorial area. One of the most valuable things any country can own is the air space above it, right? And the 'space' space. That scrap of territory, way up high, where a geosynchronous satellite can sit, that little piece of the Clarke Belt. That's worth a serious amount of money. A country able to exploit that can become very wealthy, very fast.''

"Like Tonga did,'' Megan said, "before the turn of the century. They sold off their rights to the satellite companies, a piece at a time.''

"That's right. Well, conditions have changed a little since then. But the problem now is that the big companies and the big countries still have pretty much of a hammerlock on the management of space. Near space, anyway, work in low Earth orbit—LEO—and higher, the 'geosynch' positions at 17,500 miles. You want to put a satellite up there, or fix a broken one, you have to use the shuttle via NASA, or Ariane via ESA, or Energiya via the Russians, or one of the newer companies that have formed up over the last ten years to service the big corporations. If you're a little country, though, either those people are completely out of your league—you can't afford them at all—or else you can just manage to work with them, but as part of the price for their cooperation they demand a big slice of your space rights for themselves. Those big companies can be very clever . . . and very ruthless. They don't care about some little country's future social and economic development. They care about getting control of a valuable resource and keeping it for themselves, and if you don't play ball with them, that's just too bad."

Rigel leaned back on one elbow. "But think about this. Once you're out of the gravity well, everybody's pretty much equal, and the battle goes, not to the biggest and strongest but the nimblest and most maneuverable. If you're a little country with a little fleet of space jeeps, even just a few, that means that you don't have to rely on the big companies or the big countries for your maintenance anymore. You base your staff out of the second space station, the international commercially funded one, and take care of repairs on your own satellites yourself. Cut out the middleman. After that you start making enough money from your birds to finance your own little space program. It's not that hard anymore. The technology has been available 'off the shelf' for nearly thirty years now. Yes, the big countries have been trying to keep a stranglehold on it and make all comers work through them. But the space jeep is the first crack in that wall. They know that," Rigel said, and grinned a little, "and that's why McDonnell-Boeing is so mad at me."

He looked as if he enjoyed it. Megan grinned a little in sympathy. "It's the beginning of a new life for some of the poorest countries," Rigel said. "Sub-Saharan Africa, in particular. They're sitting on a vast swath of 'space rights' that the big companies and space organizations have been taking off them, a piece at a time. Now that the jeep is becoming a reality, they're looking at pooling their resources and possibly opening their own space station, their own repair-and-resources facility. One country down there is already looking at installing a five-mile-long induction catapult, right on the equator, to put payloads into LEO without needing chemical boosters at all . . . and jeeps will boost those payloads into higher orbits when they need to go there. The African countries will be able to service their own satellites and other people's, and make enough money for their own low-cost reusable boosters. They won't be dependent on other countries and companies with other agendas. They can turn their resources to where they'll do them some good. Weather satellites to help predict famine weather, space-based ground-resource trackers to help them know where their own exploitable mineral resources are, where groundwater is hiding. Some of them will get a surprise," he said, rather softly. "They're going to find that they're too successful and too busy to carry on the wars with old tribal enemies that have been going on for centuries."

Megan wondered about that. Most of the politics she had had contact with in her short life made her think that people had an unexpected ability to be angry with each other, for stupid reasons, for centuries. "It would be nice if that happened," she said.

Rigel looked at her with one eyebrow up. "Well, skepticism is healthy in the young, they say. Just don't let it cripple you. I know, when these people find themselves in conflict over new issues, other resources, the fights can start all over again. But at least there's some hope that new arguments will have more easily visualized solutions than the old ones. People get so stuck. They forget how to look over the hill and see something new."

Megan sat back in the sand and looked at Rigel as he gazed toward the line where blue sky met blue sea. There it was, the thousand-mile glance that her father talked about sometimes, the visionary's look. It was a little scary. Megan shivered.

"You're getting cold," Rigel said. "Here, take my sweater."

He fished it out of the pile of stuff he'd brought with him and handed it to her. Megan shrugged into it. "Anyway," he said, "when I think about making a difference on that kind of scale, I don't feel guilty anymore. And there are a lot more possibilities out there than just the equatorial ones. Some of them seem pretty wild now, but in ten or fifteen years they won't. These jeeps may make it cost-effective, for the first time, to really think about terraforming Mars, making it livable for people. Mars doesn't have much infrastructure." He grinned. "No roads, no runways, no landing pads. But with jeeps, you don't need them. We're working on fuel-cell systems that will allow Mars settlers to crack water for power. If you can mine what water we know is buried on Mars, or even the cold comets that pass through on their way around the Sun, then you've got huge amounts of potential fuel that you don't have to drag up out of a gravity well."

She nodded, and stretched in the big baggy sweater. "But when you come to play in your dreams," she said, "you don't go to space. You come here."

"For the moment I only work in space," Rigel said. "What, am I supposed to think about that stuff all the time? That's the quickest way to run out of ideas . . . spend all your time in one spot. You have to move away from familiar territory to get a real sense of where you are."

"Looking at things from a different angle," Megan said.

"The binocular vision of the soul," said Rigel, with some satisfaction. "And in the land of the monocular, anyone who can see with more depth has an advantage. And they're more likely to be able to teach other people to do it, too."

"I'd love to see where you play," Megan said, a little wistfully.

Rigel smiled. "Why shouldn't you? Drop by the center tomorrow, and I'll tell them to authorize your implant for that. You should at least see the archaeo-reef . . . it's worth seeing, believe me. Are you checked out for SCUBA?"

"Actually, yeah," Megan said. "My brothers and I went to the Keys on a school trip last year and dived some of the old 'built-reef' wrecks there, the *USCG Jackson* and so on. I'll have to call home and get the diving certificate numbers for them, though . . . I didn't bring them with me."

"Okay, you do that. No, hang on to the sweater. You can give it back to me tomorrow."

He got up, stretched again, and looked out at the water. "You're going to laugh at me," he said, "but I think this is the happiest I've been since the Christmas they gave me my first train set."

Megan could believe it. "What time's good for you?" she said.

"Any time the sun's up," Rigel said, "you'll find me here. Or out in there." He waved at the bay.

"Okay. Thanks, Mr.—Jake."

"Thank you," he said, and then added as Megan started to take the sweater off again, "Hey, no, really, don't bother! Tomorrow's fine. Or leave it at your villa, put a note on it, and one of the staff'll bring it back." He waved at her. "Tomorrow sometime . . ."

He reached for his notepad, as Megan walked away, and started making notes. She was a long way down the beach before she paused to turn and look back. He was sitting there hunched over, writing hard, like a schoolkid doing his homework, intent and oblivious, and she could just barely see that he was still grinning.

Now, there, she thought, *is somebody that the money hasn't hurt. How can people come out so differently when you give them billions of dollars? Does it have something to do with what Dad was talking about? That Jake is making something, and Wim's dad is just using things, not really making anything?*

She watched a moment more, then put those thoughts aside and turned back the way she had been going, to the villas. More important now was to plan exactly how she and Wim would manage things tonight. First, though, she needed to make a couple of calls. . . .

• • •

Once back at the villa she dug around among her dad's things, found the "laptop," and took it into the upstairs bathroom with her. Then, as an afterthought, she got the boom box, brought it in, too, and turned it on while starting the water running in the tub. *Let them think I like nice music with my bath*, she thought, looking around suspiciously at the walls. It was amazing how paranoia could began creeping up on you in a situation like this. She found herself becoming less and less certain that the bathrooms, despite what the villa "guide" said on the subject of Areas of Absolute Privacy, did not have some kind of monitoring device tucked away in them somewhere.

Meanwhile, while the tub ran, Megan sat on the couch in the corner of the bathroom (it was that big a bathroom) and turned on the laptop, bringing up its satellite link. It was all astonishingly discreet. Apparently the satellite antenna was buried in the case of the laptop itself—nothing to erect, nothing to show. The link "eye" which spoke to her implant was buried in the case. She angled her neck down toward it, tilted her chin up a little—

That sudden darkening like an impending sneeze, and suddenly she was in a dark, unconfigured virtual space, hanging there as if disembodied. *Okay*, she thought. "Net contact," Megan said to the computer.

"Name?" its comms system said.

"Mark Gridley."

"Connecting."

—And suddenly she was looking at Mark, sitting in another chair somewhere else—a wiry boy of fourteen, dark-haired, with those sharp dark eyes of his. There was no background showing, just a backdrop of complete blackness. Generally Mark did not spend his time on fancy workspaces, just fancy programming.

"Megan! Didn't expect to hear from you so soon. Thought you'd still be out eating yourself into a decline."

She smiled wryly at that. "It got boring."

He gave her a look that suggested it was bad form to lie to people right to their faces. Then his eyebrows went up. "They've reprogrammed your implant," Mark said.

Megan blinked at that. "How can you tell?"

"I synched the laptop to the implant's default readings before you left," Mark said. "The live linkage right now confirms it." He gazed off into the middle distance for a moment. "Slick," he said then. "They've got it fixed so that any out-of-Xanadu Net contact restores the implant to the default settings."

Megan flushed hot. "Oh, crud! Have I screwed it up now?"

"You would have," said Mark, "if anyone but me was on the other end of this business. Fortunately, it's no big deal. Lots of programs and facilities these days use the live link to reprogram people's implants slightly for the duration of a contact. It's like the old 'cookies' that old-fashioned websites used to send people's computers to identify them and set them up for specific uses. I can keep it from defaulting."

Megan's eyes widened a little. "Can you do some reprogramming of your own? I need more access."

"To what in particular?"

"Well," she said, "everything."

He looked off into the distance again for a moment. "Give me a moment," he said, and for a moment Megan saw what he saw, lines and lines and lines of code streaming past. Mark made a face. "Inelegant," he said.

"Huh?"

"They've left a lot of blank spaces in their general authorization code," he said. "Room to put things in later, as it were. Not a good move. Wastes bytes." He stopped the scrolling code at one point and added, "And makes it easy to see where the encrypted parts of the code are. Let me get a routine working on this—"

The code streamed past again, and Mark turned away from it. "Five minutes," he said. "It's just a twenty-four bit satchel. Not unmanageable, though; there's nothing too involved. It's enough to discourage casual tampering. But I hardly qualify as 'casual.'"

Megan swallowed. "Not unmanageable" could mean all kinds of things from Mark Gridley. The son of Net Force's director had long been accepted as a kind of force of nature

in the organization, someone they couldn't stop from partici-
pating, since no one knew any way to keep him out of any information he was interested in getting into. One of Meg's other
Net Force Explorer buddies had suggested to her that this was
because Mark was really only Jay and Anna Gridley's adopted
child, the boy having actually been raised in the wild by a pack
of feral Cray 8000 supercomputers. Obviously this explanation
had to be nonsense, but it was still the best one Megan could
come up with to explain Mark's unnerving expertise with
every kind of computer under the sun. He grinned. "So you
find out anything useful yet?"

"This fast? Not a chance," Megan said. "But we'll see
what comes up tonight."

"And is that the imperial 'we,' " said Mark, "or is someone else involved?"

She told him very briefly about Wim, and about his father's
problem. Mark whistled softly. "So," Megan said, "it's as
good an excuse as any to start things rolling. I'm going to try
an intervention tonight." She could not quite bring herself to
say "break-in."

Mark put his eyebrows up. "Not much chance of getting
a lot of useful information your first time out."

She sighed. "I know. But a test run'll be useful. How quick
we get caught will tell us something about how good their
security is. It won't hurt my cover. I'm going to let them
think this is some kind of 'youthful indiscretion' that Wim
suckered me into."

"You mean you're going to let them think you're sweet
on him," Mark said in as clinical a voice as he might have
used to describe some kind of software fault.

Megan made a face. "Let them see what they think is there,
and they won't bother looking for anything more complex.
Meanwhile, if we get lucky and find something useful—"
She shrugged.

Mark snickered. "Better hope he doesn't have a different
definition than you do for 'getting lucky.' "

"Belieeeeeeve me," Megan said, "he's never going to get
that lucky. And besides, I don't think the thought will have
even crossed his mind. Fortunately."

Mark said nothing for a moment. "Aha," he said then. "Got it. Boy, somebody over there thinks his encryption is hot stuff. Oh, look, he's done this bit, too, let's let the machine work on that."

"Did you find what you were after?"

"I found a bit that says 'access all areas,' " Mark said. "So I've enabled that for you. Now what's this?" He paused again, looking at a piece of the implant programming code that was decrypting itself in front of them in bright red letters in the air. "That's interesting. They've nondefaulted your pain settings in here."

"I noticed that," Megan said. "Sometimes I still think I can feel my scalp burning from that volcanic ash."

"Limbic flashback or something similar," said Mark, sounding clinical again. "It won't last. But let me put your defaults back the way they should be—Right. Fairly simple, that. No one should depend so much on their encryption that they think they can leave command syntax options written in plain text in their code." He made a slightly unbelieving face. "What are they teaching programmers in these schools . . . ? But never mind. Any other little problems you need solved?"

"World hunger?" Megan said. "The meaning of life?"

Mark gave her a look. "I'm solving those locally at the moment," he said. "The global solutions will be along shortly. Call and let me know how it turns out."

"Will do," Megan said, and closed down the link. She shut the laptop, looked up . . .

. . . and saw that water was running over the edge of the bathtub and out onto the floor.

Megan shrieked.

Many bath towels later, Megan finished cleaning up. She shut down and put away the laptop and the boom box, had a bath (for the appearance of things), and then came downstairs and had dinner in the villa, with her dad. He was in a cooking mood and feeling playful since he'd found that the fridge suddenly contained several superb filets of beef. "Your fan again?" he'd said to Megan. She thought of Milish. It would be like him to send it. The meat was a pleasant change after all the fish lately. Afterward, Megan told him she was going for a walk on the beach, and she made her escape around eight-thirty. Her dad was already yawning and suggesting that he was going to turn in early, which suited her perfectly.

Sunset was prolonged and splendid, but she got a surprise after it, not really remembering how fast night falls in the Caribbean. She knew as a matter of science that twilight got shorter the closer you got to the equator. All the same, when the sun went down, compared to twilight in the DC area, it was as sudden as if someone had dropped a curtain: boom! The light intensity and quality changed within a matter of seconds, almost like someone had thrown a switch. A sky that had been all hot crimson, streaked here and there with fierce blue, suddenly turned a soft, pewtery, silvery beige, with a line of hot peach-color where the sun had just ducked under the water, and that too faded away to tarnished gold, then to pale silver, and at last to nothing, while the sky began to darken down to indigo.

Now, if this is anything like my last visit down this way, the bugs will come out, Megan thought. But they didn't. She strongly suspected that if she asked about this, the answer would be that the islands' builders had been careful not to bring any. *That alone*, Megan thought, *would make me think about saving for the rest of my natural life to come back here some summer.* She was not a big bug fan.

She stood there in the darkness and the sound of rushing surf for a long time before Wim finally came along, a shadow moving through shadow. "That you?"

"Yeah," she said. "What took you so long?"

"Dinner with the accountants," Wim said.

"Sounds exciting."

"Please," he said. "Where to now?"

"Upstairs. We can use our Net suite."

They slipped quietly in and up the stairs. Megan could hear, very faintly, the sounds of her father's snores coming from the main bedroom, its door standing open a crack. She and Wim tiptoed past and into the Net suite, and shut the door.

There was a spare chair recessed into the back wall. Megan went to it, pulled it free, and towed it out to where Wim could line up his own implant with the Net center. "I take it you don't think anyone noticed you leaving," Megan said.

"No. My dad doesn't care . . . he's too busy trying to patch up the corporate end of things anyway."

"How's that coming?" Megan said.

"I'm not sure," Wim said. "Some of the accountants flew in to see him, like I said. I think they were nervous about saying what they had to say even over a secure link. If news of what they were planning to do—their ideas for saving the company, I mean—if that gets out to the markets, the nervous way the business gurus are right now, it could make things a lot worse."

"By the way," Megan said, "I meant to ask you. Did you find out the names of the people who were helping your dad with his fittings?"

"One guy with some kind of Eastern name. The other one was named MacIlwain."

"Was the first one 'Nasil' something?"

"Yeah, I think so."

Megan thought about that.

"So what're we going to do?" Wim said as he sat down, looking uneasy.

"What any normal kid in our circumstances would do," said Megan. "Snoop."

She sat there in the main chair and lined up her implant, waiting for the "sneeze." . . .

It came, and after it happened, Megan looked around her in some slight surprise, for the room, or at least three walls' worth of it, still seemed to surround them. She stood up, looking out the fourth wall, where a dark plain stretched out and away in front of them. As she looked at it, it seemed less dark. It became a nighttime replica of the whole Xanadu island, with map "labels" burning here and there above the virtual versions of various buildings. Administration . . . Sports . . . General Information . . . Dining . . . Entertainment . . .

"Administration?" Wim said softly.

"Sounds like a fair bet."

They started walking. The distances between them and the

buildings were virtual, and went by with unnatural speed, so that very quickly they were standing outside a replica of the main building, brightly "lit" inside and silhouetted against the night sky. This replica had what the real one didn't—a number of doors staggered around the front of it and leading around the sides, each separately marked as the buildings on the "map" had been: Cashier, Billing, Villa Services, Restaurant Reservations, Pavilion Design . . .

They were all virtual entrances to different areas in the administrative "suite," Megan knew. She started to walk around the building, finding one thing very strange—the sound of a band playing, the kind that featured steel drums and someone banging on a cowbell. "What the heck is that?" Megan said as they walked softly around the "building."

"Didn't you read the 'rap sheet' for tonight?" Wim said. He meant the list of daily activities that appeared each morning in the villas. "They're having something called a 'limbo band.' "

"Real over-seventies stuff," Megan said. "Probably they echo it in for effect. . . ."

They made their way around the back of the "building." Here were more doors, on either side of the area with the big glass floor-to-ceiling windows that looked out on the back garden. General Recreation, Support Services, Maintenance and Repair . . . and set in the middle of the glass, a door marked STAFF ONLY.

Megan eyed this thoughtfully, wondering what her next move should be—until, very much to her surprise, Wim went straight up to this and pushed it open, for all the world as if he felt he had the right to be there. Megan hung back a little, half reluctant to touch it. *What if my contact with that door makes it plain that something a little unusual's been done to my implant?* she thought. But Wim was holding the door for her—a sudden access of old-fashioned manners that startled Megan into following him.

There was no sign of anyone physical inside the door, where what seemed a copy of the control facility lay before them. Wim was glancing around him with surprise. "No one here . . ."

But Megan wondered about that.

"Why isn't someone in here?" Wim muttered. "That doesn't make sense. What if someone's in their pavilion late at night and something goes wrong with it?"

"Yeah," Megan said. But at the same time she also wondered whether Wim was seeing things in here quite the same way she was, and she couldn't believe he was. He would much sooner have commented on it than on the mere lack of people. As she looked around at the machinery, which had been perfectly solid and normal looking the other day, Megan found that she could see through some of it—not seeing the machines' actual insides, but their virtual ones: outlines filled with streaming code, the expression of what the consoles and computers were doing in the virtual world.

Wim was walking among the machines now with that complete arrogant assurance of his, ignoring them, plainly looking for people. Megan moved more slowly behind him, looking at the machines. Concentrating, she could see more than each one's specific business going on. She could see the interconnections between them, lines of dull or burning light expressing the master network, the lines brightening as data flowed, dimming down where it paused. It was like walking through a spider's web, but the strands didn't break; a web that thickened toward the center of the network into almost a solid structure of light. Megan stood there for a moment as Wim went his way, pausing at the center of it all. It was beginning to impinge on her hearing, too, now, a hum like bees, the light reaching off in all directions, fetching up against the edges of the virtual "control room" and rebounding—

The hum got louder as Megan turned, looking around her, fascinated by the display. Light, red, golden, green, vivid blue, all the lines tight and ordered, streaking out, reaching back in—

—*except what's that one doing?* she thought suddenly. One thin pale line of very deep blue light, almost impossible to see, reaching out and away from the center of all this, reaching to the walls like all the other lines of light, but not stopping there. It pierced the walls, heading out into—"Wim!" Megan said. "Do you see this—"

That was when the alarm went off.

They both froze, staring at each other in shock. *Oh, jeez, what did we do?* Megan thought. *Unless, oh, no, just coming in that door, a timer or something and it—*

Wim bolted for the virtual door through which they had entered, but it was too late for that as well. The big slab of glass slid shut in front of them and locked with a sound like an expensive armored flyer making itself secure.

"Right," said a voice behind them—female, very cool, and very annoyed. "Maybe one or the other of you would like to explain this?"

It was Norma Wenders. She was suddenly standing there in evening clothes, flowing white striped strikingly in black, but the formal gown and the jewels she wore did nothing to make her look anything less like a silvery-blond Valkyrie minus her battle-ax, but willing to make do with bare hands in an emergency . . . which this had become.

"Uh," Megan said, and then decided that being quiet and letting the situation develop a little further might be wise.

"Uh," Wim said. "My father said—"

"—nothing about entering the virtual facility by a door labeled Staff Only," Ms. Wenders said. "Don't get yourself in any deeper than you are. Nor expect the mere fact of who he is to cut you any slack. And as for you," she said, looking at Megan, "I saw trouble written all over you the minute you came in here. And sure enough, you both prove it at once by coming in that door. We leave that there just for bright little types like you . . . didn't you suspect that? Honestly, it amazes me that anyone can be so dumb, but the world is full of these little ironies. You have one chance to explain what you thought you were doing."

"We just wanted to see—" Megan said.

"—my dad's pavilion, how it was coming," Wim said.

"Ah. That explains why you felt the need to sneak in the back way," Wenders said.

"He wasn't going to let me see it if I came in by the front," said Wim, rather rebelliously.

"And I would agree with him about that," said Ms. Wenders. "Privacy—isn't that something that people have a right to, even in their own families? Or is this one of those cultural things? Not that I care.''

She looked ice-blue murder at both of them. ''Get back to your villas. Your separate villas. Stay there. I'll be talking to your parents at the earliest opportunity.''

Everything went black.

A moment later they were sitting in the Net suite again. Wim glared at Megan. ''Well, that was a lot of no good.'' He got up, yanked the Net suite door open, stormed out.

Megan could only sit there, for the moment. *Oh, boy, oh, boy, have I blown it. What is Mr. Winters going to say . . . ?*

Yet at the same time, the image of that single dim line of light leading out of the main network, leading somewhere . . . somewhere else . . . would not let her be.

Megan went straight to bed, but it was a long, long time before she got to sleep.

When she finally awoke the next morning, her dad was nowhere to be found, but there was a rather stiff-looking note from him on the kitchen table:

Stop by the seminar room this morning. We need to talk.
                                                          Dad

I bet I know about what, Megan thought, feeling glum. Wenders had gotten at him. *Just what I needed. I come here to do a job . . . and I blow it before I even get started. It's just not fair. . . .*

She put her head into the refrigerator, having little appetite for anything but cereal and milk at the moment. As she pulled out the milk, she found another plate with a note on it. This one had a cream cheese over which rich, thick, plain cream had been poured, and the whole business was surrounded by mounds of perfect small wild strawberries. The note said:

At least eat the strawberries. M.

''All right, all right,'' she muttered, and sat down with the milk and her bowl of cornflakes, over which she strewed the strawberries. Megan then concentrated on eating the cereal as slowly as possible, but finally she realized that postponing what was going to happen wasn't making her feel any better. *I might as well get it over with*, Megan thought. *It sounds like he's going to tear a few strips off me, but waiting won't make it any better.*

She finished breakfast, went out, and found her bike parked where she had left it. It looked suspiciously shiny. It had been cleaned overnight. *Sheesh, these people . . .* she thought. If this was something you learned to expect when you were rich—the constant, slightly nervous attention to every tiny detail—she wasn't sure she liked it. Life should have a little room for comfortable slovenliness, a little slack for things to stay the way they were before someone came along to tidy them up.

As she wheeled the bike off the gravel in front of the villa and mounted up, she heard more shouting coming from over by the Dorfladen villa. Dorfladen Senior was in a snit about something. Again, Megan could bet she knew what. *I hope Wim doesn't get grounded or something*, she thought. *This wasn't his fault, after all. I talked him into it. . . .*

She sighed and rode down the lane, trying to pay a little attention to the surroundings. They were beautiful, but again, she found that the manicured, perfectly tended quality of the beauty was beginning to annoy her. Not a blade of grass seemed out of place. The palms were looking too symmetrical. She had an irrational urge to get off the bike, go over to one of those trees, and give it a good shake to see if she could disarrange something . . . then to hide in the bushes and see how long it took for someone to come along and put the leaves back the way they were "supposed to be."

She sighed and pedaled on through the balmy morning. When she got to the seminar building, Megan slipped in very quietly, expecting to find the class well under way, but to her surprise, from the sound of his voice echoing up through the hall from the seminar room's open door, it sounded as if her dad was just getting started. Also, there were Xanadu staff setting up some rolling tables with coffee and snacks out in the front atrium as she passed through, suggesting that her dad was about to give the ''students'' a break. He must have been rescheduled again. *That's not going to do his temper any good, either. . . .*

She slipped into the back of the room and sat down quietly. The place wasn't very full, which was just as well. She knew that when her father did this kind of seminar, he preferred small, intimate groups to a big crowd, half of which would lose attention within minutes. Normally he also preferred working in a circle, or around a big table, or even just curled up on a couch with everyone else sprawled in whatever position they found most conducive to comfortable conversation. He didn't have that here, but at least the participants had shown up.

They were a mixed group: a couple of bored-looking young men in their twenties, a few middle-aged ladies very well dressed and bejeweled—too much so for just after breakfast, Megan would have thought—and some older people who were more quietly dressed, several men, and another woman. One of the middle-aged ladies was currently speaking, waving one hand graciously as she spoke, as if completely unconscious of the fact that the hand in question featured several diamonds half the size of golf balls. ''Oh, but you know what they say,'' she was saying, ''that everyone has a book in them.''

''Maybe so,'' said her father, amiably enough. ''But then, everyone has a spleen in them, too. The first problem is getting it out in one piece. Then, afterward, you have to work out whether it might have been better off left where you found it.''

Megan stifled a snicker. The people in the front row stared at her dad.

The lady with the diamonds made a restrained ha-ha-ha sound that suggested her mother had told her never to laugh with her mouth open. ''Oh, Mr. O'Malley, you're such a wit. Just as in your books. It must be wonderful to live such a life. If I weren't in my present position and I didn't have so much to do, I'd like to be a writer.''

Uh-oh, Megan thought. *There it is . . . the line he's been waiting for.*

Her father smiled a sad smile. "You know how that makes me feel?" he said. "It makes me feel like you just announced that you want to start a career in sewer maintenance."

A kind of uneasy stir went through the room, the kind produced by people who don't believe someone has really said what's just come out of someone's mouth. "The comparison's exact," her father said, starting to pace. "This is an awful job. Let's leave the money out of it, since that's plainly not a concern to anyone here, though it does tend to be work that's poorly paid for many years. It's also difficult work, often unpleasant, usually lonely, often ineffective no matter how hard you work at it, frequently disruptive to family life, hard to explain rationally to other human beings whether you're enjoying it or not, almost always misunderstood by them, and, even at the best of times, equivocal as to results. In these ways, writing as a career is missing almost all of the things most people seem to look for in their work."

He looked up at the shocked faces with a rather wicked expression. "You're all saying to yourselves now, 'God, he's trying to talk us out of this.' Yes, I am! I try to talk all my writing classes out of it because I see the prospect of them going through what I went through, and possibly—about nine times out of ten—not being able to hack it, and putting themselves through a lot of anguish and hair-tearing for nothing. I'd like to spare them that, if possible, and so I try to tell them what it's like. . . ."

He looked out across the faces, as if looking for some specific reaction . . . and then began to laugh softly. "And you know what? None of them ever believes me. Any more than you folks do." He shook his head.

"Look," Megan's father said. "I meet a lot of people, doing author signings and so forth. A statistically significant number of them say to me, 'I want to be a writer.' Mostly people who say that are thinking about the sidelights of writing, the perks. Lots of money (they think!), an 'easy' lifestyle where you get to work at home and 'be your own boss,' autograph sessions, book tours . . . They don't see the awful hours you wind up working, the frustration even if you're successful, the unceasing battle with the daily world to get the work done despite endless interruptions. Not to mention the difficulty explaining this lifestyle to your family, most of whom think you really should never have given up your day job. I simply try to spare people this trouble. Mostly they walk away nodding their heads and thinking to themselves that I'm just trying to keep them out of the business, so as to make for less competition.'' He laughed, a slightly helpless sound.

"But the other ten percent still give me hope. They're the ones who just say, 'I want to write.' And that's what they do. They don't need me to encourage them. They couldn't stop if they wanted to. No discouragement from me would stop them, either. They just go home and do it.''

His listeners were shifting in their comfortable seats. Megan smiled very slightly and sat back in her chair, knowing where this was going. "Here's the bottom line,'' said her father. "If you can be discouraged, you should be, to spare you unnecessary suffering. Isn't there enough of that on the planet already, for pity's sake? And if you won't believe those of us who've been through it, if you can't be discouraged, then you'll go ahead and write, and good luck to you. And I wish you every success.''

He stopped and looked up at them good-naturedly. His listeners looked at him, some of them with expressions suggesting that they were nervous about what might happen next.

"That's the bad news,'' her father said, fairly cheerfully. "Let's take a break. They'll be putting out coffee and snacks up in the entry atrium. When we've all had a little something, and if you're still determined to write, we can settle down again and talk about the different kinds of writing you're interested in doing, get at the mechanics of them, and what the immediate challenges are. Let's meet again in . . . twenty minutes? Fine. Last one out, close the door behind you, if you would. . . .''

Megan watched the ''students'' file out past her, some looking amused, a couple looking angry, some of their expressions simply seeming more confused than anything else. She had seen that confusion on her dad's workshoppers before, and knew what it meant. Maybe a tenth of them would survive to the third day. Maybe none. And if anyone made the mistake of somehow shifting her father into genuinely critical mode, Pompeii would probably seem mild by comparison.

He stood down there in the "pit," watching them go, and then glanced up at her and sat down.

Megan got up and headed down to him.

"How's it going?" Megan said.

He looked up at her from underneath his eyebrows, a sure trouble sign. "Not as well as I would have hoped," her father said, "especially as regards you."

Uh-oh. "Daddy, I—"

"Don't 'Daddy I' me. Megan, you've embarrassed me. Seriously. I had a very annoyed visit from Norma Wenders this morning."

Oh, crap. She actually came over? "What did she say?"

"She told me that you and what's-his-name, young Wim, were involved in an attempted security breach last night. Megan, what were you thinking of?"

"Dad, we were just curious. We only wanted to—"

"I really don't want to hear it at this point! You knew perfectly well that you had no business being where you were. And after these people extended you the courtesy of being here in the first place, you abuse their courtesy like this? I had hoped I'd raised you better."

Her dad had to know exactly what she'd been up to. What was this about—was he mad she'd gotten caught? Nothing to do now except play it humble. "Uh, I'm sorry."

"I wish I was more certain about that. The Xanadu people have extended us a tremendous opportunity here. Under normal circumstances, neither of us would ever have been able to afford a couple of weeks in a place like this. Not even a couple of days. These people go out of their way to be nice to me by letting you come along—and then you pull this kind of stunt! I'm mortified. God knows whether they'll ever want me back here again. I'm sure they won't want you."

Megan flushed hot with sudden fear. *Oh, no, they're not going to deport me, are they? I won't have found out anything, Mr. Winters'll—*

"They have the right to send you straight home if they like," her father said. "Fortunately for you, I was able to talk Ms. Wenders out of it. She was certainly in favor of the idea, but after a while she thought she could write it off as a youthful excess. Also, apparently someone else she had talked to earlier was very upset at the thought of you leaving. Jacob Rigel."

"Oh," Megan said. *Saved by a chance conversation on the beach . . . !*

"He seems to think you're worth talking to, anyway," her father said. "He's asked them to go over your implant and enable it for his pavilion. That was something Ms. Wenders wanted to check with me. I told her it was all right. As long as you behave," her father said as Megan opened her mouth. "I don't want you getting caught doing anything like that again. You understand me?"

There was something about that wording that Megan found interesting, but she wasn't going to bring up the subject just now. "Uh, yeah. I mean, yes, Dad."

"Good. Now give me a hug and tell me you'll be good after this," her father said.

Megan went over and hugged him, though the second part of the sentence made her raise her eyebrows. It wasn't the sort of thing she'd ever heard out of her father in a long time, since apparently he had given up on the concept years before. While she was hugging him, he said in her ear, so softly that even she could hardly hear him, "Think that was convincing enough?"

Megan blinked in surprise. "Uh-huh," she said, as softly, and smiled just a little. Once again she realized that the older she got, the smarter her father got as well. It was enough to restore her faith in human nature.

"Good," her dad said aloud, and patted her back, and then pushed her away a little, taking her by the shoulders and shaking her slightly. "So you behave, then."

"Okay, Dad," she said, keeping the grin off her face by sheer force of will. *Staged*, she thought. *He's wasted as a writer. He should be acting.*

"So what are you going to do with the rest of your afternoon?" her father said.

"I don't know," Megan said, and thought a moment. "I should go take care of that implant . . . and then I guess I might go see the resident foodie. He keeps sending me all this stuff; it seems rude not to thank him."

"You go ahead, then. And stay out of trouble."

Megan went off, feeling more than usually thoughtful.

She made her way to the main facility and walked through it with a rather guilty air. It was not exactly as if the people there were staring at her, but she caught some sidelong looks and some disapproving expressions as she made her way back to the programming and control department. Once there, she stood up on the railed part and looked around, again rather guiltily, for some familiar face.

"Hey, Megan," came a voice from behind her. "How's tricks?"

She turned. It was Len, making his way down to the "downstairs" level with a bundle of data storage solids. "Uh," she said, thinking of several answers, none of which would be particularly funny today. "I, uh . . . I was looking for Ms. Wenders."

"She's not here," said Len. "Out to lunch."

"Oh." That at least was a slight relief. "Hey, look, uh, I just want to say I'm sorry about last night."

Len glanced around him as if making sure no one was listening, then chuckled. "Look," he said, "it's no skin off our noses. We don't mind. Life around here can get boring sometimes."

Nasil came up from the lower level at that point and gave Megan an amused look. "The criminal returns to the scene of the crime. . . ."

"Yeah, well, I'm really sorry."

"Megan, forget it," Nasil said. "It's not important. I don't think you came here just for that, though."

"She didn't?" Len said.

Nasil elbowed him. "Sadist. Don't forget, she's got to get her implants tweaked. The Reef."

Megan swallowed. She did not want anything done to her implant at the moment. Who knew what Mark had done to it?—and how visible it would be to anyone tweaking her implant. "Uh, I'll pass for just now. Actually, besides apologizing abjectly, I was looking for Milish."

"Oh, he's in the usual location. Running around ranting, raving, screaming at the kitchen staff, doing chef things."

Megan nodded. "Listen," she said. "I did that sample pavilion the other day. . . ."

"Yeah, Pompeii. How was it?"

"Uh, very effective." She swallowed and clasped her hands to keep herself from scratching accidentally. "Look, I was just wondering . . . do you ever get people flipping out?"

"Why? Because the scenario's too overwhelming?"

She nodded.

He looked at her and didn't say anything for a moment. "Not as a rule," Nasil said then, a little more softly than he had before. "Did you perceive that as a possible problem?"

"No, not really. Not for me, anyway. But I was thinking that maybe occasionally someone might have a reaction to, say, having gotten away from it all too completely. More completely than they'd originally planned."

Nasil shook his head. "This probably isn't widely known," he said, "but in the setup questionnaire we send out when someone first books here, there's a psychiatric profiling package. It's fairly subtle. People have to do it for the insurance coverage, and no one seems to mind. But that questionnaire has occasionally led us to . . . well, we never reject a client. We might redirect them. And if they don't redirect real well, well, we may just not be able to work out mutually suitable dates. You know what I mean?"

"Uh, I think so," Megan said.

"Does that answer your question?"

"More or less," she said. "I guess I may as well go see Milish. . . . Thanks."

She went out and found her way down to the doorway that led to Milish's kitchen. Far from being the peaceful haven the place had been the other day, it was a nightmare. People in white were running in all directions carrying pots and trays and yelling at each other, apparently in French, while a voice from a loudspeaker issued more instructions in French, and everywhere utensils banged, pots boiled, extractor fans howled, and pans sizzled.

Megan was about to turn right around and go back the way she came when a voice shouted from the depths of the kitchen, "Stop that girl! Don't let her get away!"

She was so astounded that she stood right where she was, half afraid that Ms. Wenders was going to materialize in front of her out of a cloud of steam. But it was only Milish who appeared a few moments later, drying his hands on a dish towel and then taking off his tall hat to tuck it under one arm and wipe his face. "Perfect," said Milish, "an excuse to escape from this hellhole. They're getting lunch ready, but they don't need me for that. Come on. We're cheesemaking today."

"What kinds?"

"Monterey Jack, cream cheese, cottage cheese, and Neufchatel," he said. "All green. Come on, the dairy's down the hall and out the back."

They walked out and down a hallway, into another room that had, arranged along its walls, a number of large stainless-steel vats. All their contents were white. "I don't get it," Megan said, glancing at them as they passed. "Do you dye them later or something?"

Milish laughed. "What an innocent. 'Green' when used of cheeses means unripened. No skin, or no significant skin, is allowed to develop. A 'green cheese' is one you eat fresh, within a few days. That's what the old joke about the moon meant. People thought it looked like the kind of round, white fresh cheese that people made at home."

"Another mystery solved," Megan said, genuinely a little interested. That particular piece of folklore had puzzled her when she was little, and even when she had grown up she'd thought they meant some kind of variant on blue cheese.

"Come on back here," Milish said, "and you can see the curing room."

At the back of the large room he opened what Megan would at first have taken for a meat locker, and waved her in. "We have to keep the temperature steady at fifty degrees in here," he said, "and the humidity at forty percent exactly, otherwise the cheeses go bad in a matter of minutes. Very few people have ever successfully made cheeses in a Caribbean climate—the heat and humidity make this paradise for molds and bugs that would ruin the flavor . . . or kill you."

He shut the door and looked around them at the sides of the "meat locker," which were completely covered with wire shelving, and the wire shelving was completely covered with hundreds of cheeses of various sizes. "And now that we're out of the open," he said, "let me extend Mr. Halvarson's thanks to you for coming to help him with his problem."

Megan stared.

Milish smiled. "This is one of the few places on the island where security never installed a camera or a sound system," he said. "They tried to, but I pitched a fit. The things are magnets for dust, and dust harbors all kinds of inimical bacteria and molds, and would screw up the cheeses, I claimed."

Megan looked at him with what she suspected was a fairly cockeyed expression. "Do you mean that you kept sending me all that food because—"

"Megan—can I call you Megan?—I've been trying to get you in here for three days. I was beginning to think I'd exhausted the possibilities. Most people pig out when they get here. I don't usually see people refusing food. I was wondering if you'd started to develop some kind of psychiatric problem."

She snickered. "No," she said. "Just a reaction to the luxury, I guess."

Milish laughed, too. "Well." He studied the corners of the ceiling. "What makes me laugh," he said, "is that the security people bought my reasons. They obviously don't know that most cheesemakers depend on the local yeasts and bacteria for their results. Some can't be made at all without the local flora—they used to drag moldy horse harness through vats of Blue Vinney, I hear, to inoculate the stuff."

Megan made a face.

"Yes," Milish said, "well, it may be a myth, and you wouldn't likely get a chance to eat the real stuff, anyhow, because ninety percent of all Blue Vinney is forged these days. Never mind. Anyway, I can pass on the information Mr. Halvarson wants you to have here. We're secure—though we should make it fast, because if we don't come out pretty soon, whoever's monitoring the outside kitchen might start to suspect hanky-panky and hit a client alarm. Anyway, I'm glad you finally turned up. If you'd done it a little sooner, I could have spared you some trouble.''

Megan made a wry face.

Milish spent the next few minutes or so talking very fast indeed. ''You seem be doing all right for someone with no help,'' he said. ''Or someone who didn't know where the help was. Seize the moment, my dear, never fail to seize the moment around here.'' He elbowed Megan in a conspiratorial way. ''But try not to get caught again. They won't have any choice but to get rid of you if you do.''

''Ms. Wenders . . .'' Megan said. ''She's a hard case, huh?''

''None harder. You should have seen her before she mellowed.''

Megan swallowed. ''Have there been any more attacks that I don't know about?''

''I think not. Dorfladen's been the last one. The man may be a lout, but his stockholders didn't deserve what happened to him. At any rate, I take it you have some kind of plan to help find out who's at the bottom of all this. . . .''

''I have some ideas,'' Megan said, ''but it's going to mean getting into the system.''

''You're on your own there,'' Milish said. ''I'm no techie except as regards making hollandaise. There I can quote you the physics of the process until your eyes bleed. Here—'' He shook his head. ''The boss is a friend . . . that's the only advantage I've got. And even that's not much good if the meals are late. Which reminds me, we'd better get out of here. If I'm out of the kitchen too much just now, someone may notice. Take a cheese, any cheese.''

She picked up another of the Brie-ish-looking ones. ''Let that sit out in the air for an afternoon,'' Milish said, studying it with a practiced eye. ''No more than that, otherwise it'll get up and walk away by itself. Remember, if you need anything technical, I'll try to help. But be discreet. There's no telling who might be involved in this.''

Megan nodded. Together they went out of the locker, discussing the virtues of Melba toast for eating with a really runny cheese—'' 'Coulant' is the word, dear,'' Milish said as he ushered her out into the main kitchen again. ''Only noses are 'runny.' Enjoy it, now.''

Megan snickered as she went out with her cheese. She killed the snicker with great speed as a door opened down the hall and Norma Wenders emerged. Ms. Wenders gave Megan a look in passing. Then she glanced at the cheese, and back at Megan again, and allowed her a small wintry smile. ''Behaving yourself at last, I see,'' she said.

''Yes, ma'am,'' Megan said.

''Good. Keep it that way.''

Megan saved the smile until she was well on her way back to the villa.

When she got in, Megan found that she had her appetite back, enough of it for her to go through the refrigerator with extreme prejudice, finding out whether what Milish had been saying about the cheeses was true. It was. Some considerable amount of cholesterol later, Megan took a cold drink upstairs with her and found her dad's ''laptop,'' and the boom box, and went into the palatial bathroom again to have another ''bath.''

She shut and locked the door, and looked around her thoughtfully. Then Megan turned on the tap at a much lower flow rate, turned on the boom box, and made herself comfortable on the couch again, once more performing the little mental gesture that brought her own implant on-line.

Blink, and she was in darkness.

''Workspace, please,'' she said.

Blink, and here was her workspace, her amphitheater. She stood on the topmost row. Saturn was coming up, half full, away in the distance. One of the smaller inner moons plunged across the sky off to her left, frantically changing phase from crescent to half as she watched. Megan just stood there and looked at that for a moment, thinking of Jacob Rigel's dream. Toward the sun, in past Jupiter's orbit, past the faint chain of stars that would be the asteroid belt, lay Mars. *To start making Mars livable,* she thought. *I might live to see that happen. If what he's doing works . . .*

But why wouldn't it? It was working. That was why, as Jacob said, McDonnell-Boeing and the other big aerospace firms were so angry with him.

Megan walked down the steps of the amphitheater to where her easy chair waited. *But they* are *angry,* she thought. *And who knows . . . whether someone might not like him to have a little accident. . . .*

Megan shook her head. The paranoia of the last few days was beginning to affect her. Still, the thought would not quite go away. . . .

She sat down in her chair and thought for a moment. "Mark Gridley," she said. She was about to add "Encrypted," and then had a sudden thought. "Pause," she said.

"Waiting," said her computer's "management" voice.

If someone's imported my workspace whole . . . what's to stop them from tampering with my encryption routines? It would be a nasty little surprise. She would think her conversation was secure, when it would be no such thing.

"Complete the connection," said Megan.

"Working."

Blink, and suddenly she was looking at Mark, sitting in his chair still. *Does he ever get out into the real world?* Megan wondered, as she'd wondered before. *When does he pee?* Then she turned away from that thought, half afraid that she might at some point stumble across the answer.

"Megan," Mark said. "What's up? I'm a little rushed right now."

"Great. Can we talk?" she said.

He looked at her quizzically. "I don't know that anyone's ever been able to stop you."

"Thanks so much."

"But before you tell me anything—I'm going to send you a file. I want you to put it in this folder of your villa's Net computer when you get off this one." He showed her a tree diagram and pointed out one folder. "It's a program. Run it."

"It's not going to blow anything up, is it?"

Mark looked thoughtful. "We'll find out later," he said. "But I may need to turn up inside the Xanadu system without being noticed at some point—by either the powers that be, or whoever you're hunting—and this'll give me a hint as to how, if I can make it work out right. I'll still have to come in through the satlink—there's no way to compromise their system from the 'normal' Net access pathways, they're too well protected against that. But if this works out OK, I shouldn't have any trouble getting in to help you via the 'back door.' "

"All right," Megan said, looking at the little rotating solid which suddenly appeared in her space. "How am I supposed to get that into the main machine, though?"

"I've come up with a little more creative reprogramming for your implant," Mark said. "I can get it to act like a splitter—a bridge between the two systems. Your implant will access them simultaneously and leave each system thinking it's firewalled against the other, so no alarms will be triggered."

There was something about his voice that brought Megan up short. "You think."

"We'll find out," Mark said.

Megan sighed. She had learned that when Mark started describing things like this as reality, which to her sounded more like magic, she had to just swallow her disbelief and see what happened. He hadn't been wrong yet . . . which unnerved her somewhat, for Megan did not believe that the law of averages much liked being flouted with any kind of regularity.

"So what was it you wanted to talk to me about?" Mark said.

"The stuff you did to my implant . . ." She called up that memory again, the weblines of light, all bounded . . . but one. "This is a sealed system, isn't it."

"The pavilion system? Yup. They wouldn't dare link to anything outside. It would defeat the whole purpose."

"Well, I saw one link leading somewhere else. . . ."

Mark looked alert. "Did you, now? That could be diagnostic. Though there would be links to outside comms for business purposes. They wouldn't be attached to the main system, though."

Megan shook her head. "This didn't look like there was much bandwidth involved."

"Just something skinny?"

"Just a thread."

Mark thought about that. "A tripwire . . ." he thought. "Or just a link to something hidden. Did someone get careless, I wonder?"

"It doesn't make sense," Megan said. "If you gave me 'all areas' access, someone else must be able to see the same stuff. Why haven't they? Wenders or somebody?"

"Maybe they haven't been looking in the right places at the right times," Mark said. "Or . . ." He looked thoughtful, then grinned a little. "Some systems have system administrator levels which are never used: 'supersysadmin' levels . . . unused because most people using that system just don't know about them, or because all the administration that matters is carried out below that level. I may have enabled you higher than anybody but the Big Boss himself when I tinkered with that code." He smiled a slow odd smile. "You'll have to test it. But bear that link in mind. When we do go in, I want to look at it. I think it's meaningful."

Megan nodded.

"Meanwhile," Mark said, "why not bring the laptop in where the main Net computer is, and let's see if my little stratagem works."

Megan blinked herself out of implant contact with the machine, got up and turned off the water, and went into the Net suite with the laptop and the boom box. There she closed and locked the door, sat in the implant chair, and lined up on the Net machine.

The implant made contact. A moment later she was sitting inside her workspace, in the Net machine's version of it. She looked down at the laptop, still sitting in her lap—

Suddenly an innocent-looking little cube was tumbling in the air in front of her, the graphical representation of the program Mark wanted her to transfer. "Just 'drag' it out of the laptop and 'drop' it into the big machine—"

She nodded, and called up the machine's basic "tree" diagram, its hierarchy of file folders, until she found the one Mark had indicated. Megan got up out of her chair, plucked the cube out of the air, went over to the tree, and pushed the cube through the side of the "folder" graphic hanging there.

The folder swelled, then flattened again to show that it had accepted the program, and also showed her a list of the other files in there as well. They all had icons that made no sense at all to Megan, and she ignored them. She put her finger on the representation of the file she had just introduced, and said to it, "Run."

Then Megan flinched as the air around her abruptly filled with a nasty high squealing sound. The fabric of the whole area around her wavered a little bit, as if it was being viewed through water. Megan gulped. She had never seen her workspace do anything like this before. After a few seconds it settled, and her space got back to normal, but under everything ran a soft low-frequency hiss of white noise that would not go away.

Mark appeared in Megan's workspace, looking around him. "That's what I like about you," he said. "Other people change their workspaces every half an hour. You're dependable. Yours never changes."

Megan decided to take that as a compliment for the moment. "What's that noise?" she said.

"My scrambler," Mark said, walking over to the villa computer's tree structure and looking at it for a moment. It faded out at the top and bottom. Plainly if the whole thing were displayed at once, it would have gone straight to the vanishing points at zenith and nadir. "Did a little tinkering on it to make sure that no one 'native' to the system notices I'm here. I may have to reinforce it afterward, make it keep cycling through 'invisibility' patterns to keep repeat visits from being noticed." He grinned. "If we need many repeat visits . . . which I doubt. But another hour, another challenge."

He touched the tree directory, and it expanded straight up like Jack's beanstalk. Mark took hold of it and flipped it farther up with his hands, like someone running something up a flagpole. Abruptly he stopped and peered at one of the folders of the computer. "Did you hear some noise in here while that program was running?" he said.

"Yeah. Kind of a screech."

"Thought so. This isn't your own space, is it? It's a clone."

"Yeah."

"Well, somebody added something when they cloned it. Some eavesdropping utilities. Very nasty."

"Are they off-line now?" Megan said. That struck her as possibly a bad idea. It might alert the Xanadu mole to the fact that someone was on to him or her.

"Nope, they're in a loop," Mark said. "You might want them for later, for disinformation. They'll come back when I disconnect." He ran some more of the directory tree "up the flagpole," then stopped again.

"Aha," Mark said, and put his finger on one folder. It expanded and became a tree of considerable size itself.

"This is the gateway to the main computers," he said. "The ones that provide access to the scenarios these people build."

"The pavilions."

"Yeah. Millions of files. What a little playground." He smiled. "But later."

He poked another of the folders. It expanded in the air into a kind of frame shape, a square full of darkness. Mark peered through it. Megan looked over his shoulder.

Through the frame she could see little but various small pointy icons, pyramid-shaped—maybe hundreds of them, scattered across a dark landscape. "What're those?" she said.

Mark chuckled. "They're pavilions. After all, originally, pavilions were just tents. . . ."

"Can we go in from here and look at them?"

"Not directly. Or, not if you don't want to set off eight thousand alarms. This is the way the system sees the pavilion structures from outside. If we ventured into that landscape as we are, without the right clearances, the whole place would shut down to preserve its own integrity.'' Mark shook his head. ''But that won't take too long to sort out.''

''Mark, come on! How are you going to steal their clearances? They're supposed to have the best security in—''

Mark just smiled at her. ''It's a nice claim, isn't it?''

Megan shook her head, for she had had this thought herself, earlier. ''Publicity . . .''

''Oh, I'll bet their security is pretty good. But it can't be perfect. For one thing, they've never hired me. For another, no system this complex can be unbreakable. There's just too much code. And even leaving mistakes and loopholes out of it . . .'' Mark smiled more angelically than usual. ''There's always a back door.''

Megan said nothing to that. It had occurred to her that, to allow Xanadu to be built at all, some of the local government officials in the Bahamas who were in a position to help or hinder the project must have been offered some considerable incentives. They would have wanted some advantages for themselves, of course. And no one wants a computer system on their doorstep of this kind of power and complexity that cannot, in emergencies, be quietly infiltrated. . . .

''Anyway, you've got the implant, and the splitter's working,'' Mark said. ''There won't be any problems once we get in.''

''And don't forget Wim,'' Megan said. ''I told you how his father was trashed by whoever's doing this. He helped me get at the 'link' I saw the other night, and he's suffering for it right now. I think he has the right to come along.''

''Is he any use?''

Megan wasn't sure how to answer that. ''Maybe,'' she said. ''But anyway, he's been a help. Indirectly. We wouldn't have gotten this far without him.''

''Fair enough,'' Mark said. ''He'll have to move pretty fast to keep up, though. So will you.''

Megan took a friendly swipe at Mark's head. ''Listen, Squirt, I'm sure I can manage. You just keep your own socks pulled up. We have the honor of Net Force to think about here. Not to mention stopping anything worse happening.''

"You expecting worse?"

Megan nodded. "I think so. These things have been escalating. At first it was just theft. Then people started getting hurt. One person even died from a heart attack brought on by all this. A lot of people lost their shirts investing in one of Wim's dad's companies. All their savings wiped out in an afternoon. I don't think we should wait around to see what else happens. We should go after whoever's doing this."

"Right," Mark said. "Does he have the same implant that you've got?"

"As far as I can tell."

"Well, I'm going to have to tinker with his, too. Otherwise he's going to find himself running deaf and blind if he tries to keep up with us . . . and we won't be able to slow down for him. This system has safeguards, believe me."

Megan thought about that. "It may take a while. We'd better say tonight, then. And nighttime might be better, anyway. A lot of the guests here get together then and party, and the party area abuts onto the physical control facility. The distractions may help."

"All right," Mark said. "What time?"

Megan was tempted to say "late." That way if she got caught at something again, there might be fewer people to know about it. But at the same time something was niggling at her mind, saying, don't wait, make it sooner rather than later! "Ten o'clock local," she said.

"You're on. Call out on the laptop, just as you did now. Be on and waiting with the scrambler in place, and have Wim on his machine at the same time. Give him a copy of the scrambler, too—just mail it over to his machine, encrypted, and tell him how to install it. If your mole is active in the system, it won't be long before he or she knows we're there, so we're going to have to move really fast to get what you want. You'll have to re-create or relocate that 'link' for me so that I can use it to start hunting what you're after. But once we present that particular ticket at the door, things are going to get busy."

Mark looked around him one last time. Then, much to

Megan's surprise, he produced a feather duster and began to clean the air with it.

"Wiping the data solid for any possible traces of me," Mark said, and put the feather duster in his pocket as well. "And overwriting the medium, just to be sure."

Megan shook her head. "They should have sent you down here," she said. "You'd have found out who was doing this by now."

But Mark was shaking his head, too. "Not a chance. Everyone knows who my dad and mom are. They wouldn't have let me near anything important. You're a lot lower-profile . . . and you've done okay." The admission was not completely grudging. "You did good groundwork. Now we'll build on what you've laid down. That's what Net Force people do. Work together. There are no heroes in a team. . . ."

Megan had her suspicions about where Mark had heard that. "Okay," she said, "I'm going to go get Wim set up."

"Great. The laptop will do the work: I'll leave the implant access-cloning routine running. . . . Just sit him down in front of it. He'll get a copy of what I sorted out for you the other day."

"Good. And Mark . . ." She made one more suggestion to him about the implant defaults. "They should all be set to synchronize at intervals . . . all of them. The limbic levels in particular."

"Uh, okay." He looked briefly mystified. "I'll take care of it."

"Right," she said.

"As for you, after I get off, you might want to lay down a little 'black propaganda.' "

"I'll call home and bitch about the terrible time I'm having," Megan said, "and how everyone here hates me, and how I'm going to stay in tonight and eat myself into a decline."

"Sounds like a plan," Mark said. "Ten o'clock, then."

He vanished from her space.

Megan listened as the pink noise faded. "Call home," she said to her space.

•   •   •

It was nearly half an hour before she was able to get free of that particular connection. Her brothers were less interested in listening to her bitching than in wanting to hear about the resort. Her mother, who had just come home, was more interested in hearing about how her father was doing. She plainly missed him fiercely and wasn't happy that he wasn't available to talk to her. "I need to hear his voice," her mom said, somewhat plaintively. "Anything but four other voices screaming that no one loves them enough to take them to the world's most expensive resort, and they're disgusted to have to stay home by themselves . . ."

Megan had to laugh at that. But she was careful to plant the necessary disinformation regardless. When the call was done, she slipped out of the villa, down onto the beach, and was not particularly surprised to find Wim down there, walking back and forth and looking extremely unhappy. As soon as he saw Megan, he came hurrying toward her with that head-down-shoulders-forward walk that was normally his father's, and made you think he was about to ram you head on.

"Are you okay?" Megan said, rather hurriedly, before Wim could go into some kind of rant.

He opened his mouth, then closed it again, as if surprised. "Uh," he said, "yeah." As if it was a new idea, he then added, "How are you?"

Megan was slightly astonished. "Okay," she said, "I think. I didn't get yelled at as badly as I thought I was going to."

"I did," Wim said, sounding very glum. "Worse."

"I'm really sorry," Megan said. She was. She could imagine what the noise she had heard that morning must have sounded like close up. "But listen. You've got to come over to our villa and use my machine."

"What's your machine got that mine hasn't?"

"Don't ask right now. You've just got to come over."

"I can't. I'm grounded. I have to stay here."

"Who knows you're grounded? I mean, down there? Who would tell your father they saw you leave?"

"Uh . . ." He thought about that. "I don't know."

"Well, it doesn't matter," Megan said. "You've got to do

it. Just come on and let's get it done, because you have to get your implant geeked if we're going to have any chance of finding out who sabotaged your dad. Mine's done already. I can get in anyplace now . . . and my 'source' can do the same for you.''

Wim stared at her. "Why should he?"

"I can't tell you now," Megan said. "I may not be able to tell you later, either. Just come on!"

He stared, then nodded. They hurried into the villa together, and Megan went to find the laptop . . . then led Wim into the upstairs bathroom.

"Oh, no," he said.

She gave him an exasperated look. "This is no time to get cold feet on me," Megan said. "In!"

Wim looked at her, then went in. Megan shut the door. "Here," she said, holding up the laptop, "line up on this." But she couldn't help thinking, with somewhat angry amusement, *If they do have any listening devices in here, what are they going to make of that last line . . . ?*

Wim gulped, then looked at Megan oddly. "Did something—"

"Yes," Megan said. "Don't let's go into it now, OK? Come on."

She led him out hurriedly, dumping the laptop and picking up the boom box on the way out. Once outside the house, with the boom box running, she said, "What's your dad doing tonight?"

"Taking delivery on his pavilion. Finally."

Oh, cripes, he's going to be in there, too. Is any of this going to be easy? But Megan already knew the answer to that. "Wim, tonight's the night. Be ready."

Wim was mystified, but he nodded. "When are we going in?"

"Ten o'clock. Be up in your Net suite around ten minutes before then, and call my suite. The code should be up there in that little 'phone book' they've left downstairs in the kitchen. You know where. The drawers by the refrigerator."

"Uh . . . I haven't been in the kitchen. The cook takes care of that."

Megan covered her eyes briefly. "Good, it'll be a learning experience for you. Just stay out of the refrigerator, it may be bad for you. Whatever you do, though, be on time. Don't let anything distract you. I'm going to mail you a file. Decrypt it, then install it, and run it when we're ready to start. And lock yourself in your Net suite, if you have to."

"All right," Wim said. He turned and hurried away.

Not even a wave goodbye, Megan thought. *Maybe it is something cultural.*

She started to walk up to the villa again, but then was slightly surprised to see her father wandering down through the line of palm trees that separated the villa's grounds from the beach. She sat down there on the sand, just out of the reach of the incoming tide, and waited for him.

He was in no hurry. A few minutes passed before he was standing by her, looking out across the water. "This is really lovely, isn't it," he said.

"Yeah. How did the rest of the seminar go?"

"Not too badly," he said. "They're not a terrible group. The usual problem of egos overafflicted with money . . . but some of the 'attitude' is wearing off those egos at the corners. We'll see how they behave tomorrow."

Megan nodded.

"And how has your day been?" said her father. "After what must have been a somewhat unpropitious start."

Megan smiled. "I had a talk this morning with someone whom Halvarson apparently wanted me to meet."

"Did it help?"

"Some." Megan gulped, remembering her father telling her when all this started that maybe he didn't want to know what she was doing. At the time it had made her feel extremely adult and important. Right now it made her feel as if she were out on a limb, one that someone else might be in the process of sawing off. "Dad, do you think you can cover for me this evening?"

"Certainly," he said, sitting down in the sand beside her. "You're getting tired of all that rich food. Or of the social whirl. Or else you're just embarrassed out of your mind after what happened last night, and you've decided to stay in."

She blushed. She could still see Ms. Wenders's face, that look of cool condemnation. It was not something she particularly wanted to see again.

"So how long do you want me to stay out?" said her father.

"Late," Megan said. "Till midnight, anyhow. But you should be gone well before ten."

"That's easy enough to manage," her father said. "And you will be . . . where?"

"Upstairs in the villa. The Net suite. I have to do some surfing."

Her dad nodded. "No problem," he said. "I believe they're having a waltz night tonight. Some of my 'students' should be able to waltz . . . and after this afternoon some of them will probably welcome the chance to step on my feet."

"You're great," Megan said, and hugged him hard.

He didn't react much, just looked down at her. "So I hear," her father said. "Megan . . . is this going to be safe for you?"

She hesitated. "I think so."

"Good. Just be careful. And when you're on your way . . . good hunting." Just a twitch of a smile. "Meanwhile, let's go in again, and I'll yell at you some more."

He got up and went in. After a few moments, keeping her face scrupulously straight, even a little depressed-looking, Megan got up and went after him.

5

The rest of the afternoon was difficult for Megan. She tried to relax, but it was impossible. Going out to the beach would have been pleasant, but now she was becoming nervous that she might run into Jacob Rigel and he might want to know why she hadn't come to dive his virtual reef. Though she wanted to do it, there was no way she wanted to do it this afternoon, when her brain was humming with nervousness about the impending raid on the Xanadu system. So she hid inside the villa and conducted more raids on the refrigerator that had somehow acquired another lobster.

"They keep making these deliveries when I'm not looking," her father said to her around seven, while he was sorting through his clothes to work out what to wear to the waltz party that night. "I wonder if there isn't some kind of secret dumbwaiter connecting to an underground conveyor belt, or some such."

Megan shook her head as she went after the small jar of lime mayonnaise that had come with the lobster. "It's just people," she said. "Specialists in being unobtrusive. Like the ones who rake the gravel, and whoever keeps polishing my bike."

"Are you sure?" her father said. "Have you ever seen anyone doing it?"

He was teasing her, but there was an air of warning about his words, too, one which Megan was quick to pick up, though she doubted that anyone who didn't know her father well would have caught it. He, too, was responding to the realization that all this "unobtrusive" and near-instantaneous service meant the clients of Xanadu were being closely watched. Even if you thought the proprietors' motives were strictly benevolent, it was a little hard to take. *But I guess the really rich people are used to being watched all the time anyway*, Megan thought. *Guarded against people who want to kidnap them, or steal what they've got. . . .* The thought took a lot of the cachet out of being rich. *Whatever having heaps of money can buy you*, Megan thought, *it looks like freedom, and privacy, aren't on the list. . . .*

About eight her father was ready to go. Resplendent in his tuxedo, he stepped out the front door and said, "Lock up tight, now. I'll be back after midnight, I guess."

"Okay," Megan said. "Have fun. . . ."

She waved at him as he strolled away across the gravel and vanished down the lane, then she shut the door, locked it, and went around the villa and did the same to all the other doors.

That I know of, she thought. *Now he's got me being paranoid about secret tunnels into the house. Thank you so much, Daddy dear.*

She sighed and went upstairs to the Net suite, where for a few moments she simply stood in the doorway and looked at the discreet, beautiful, desperately expensive computer sitting there. *I said I was going to do some surfing. I suppose I could always go in and tidy up all that junk mail sitting around in my space*, Megan thought. *If anyone is watching me, that'll bore them silly.*

And so she did just that, sat down and did the internal blink that left her looking across her amphitheater at Saturn, and walked down the steps to where her work-chair sat waiting. "Okay," she said to her system. "Cleanup time . . ."

Obediently the "crate" into which she had jammed all the cyberjunk released its contents into the air, and the center-stage area of her amphitheater immediately began to resemble a playground for psychokinetic toddlers, a welter of floating bright-colored cubes, spheres, and pyramids. Some of them, having been stored without attention for some days, began yelling "Read me first! Read me first!" in tiny, insistent voices.

Megan rolled her eyes and started in. She called up a clock to keep her company, and it sat there ticking off the minutes while Megan sat cheerfully throwing away requests that she fill out questionnaires, and send off five dollars for the world's best brownie recipe, and find out how to Make Money Instantly. That one always made her snicker. If it was that easy, why wasn't the sender off enjoying himself instead of sending me random mail? Megan wondered.

She erased that mail with intense pleasure, as well as numerous others offering her real estate deals and diet drugs and ways to lose half her body weight in just six weeks. After a while she began to enjoy this sufficiently that she briefly lost track of the time, and when the air around her chimed once, the alarm she had set for herself, she looked up in surprise and saw that it was twenty to ten.

Megan picked up the "laptop," which sat waiting by the lineup chair, and shut down the workspace. Then she activated the scrambler program, linked with the laptop and with the main Net computer again, reentering her workspace, now secure . . . and waited.

Three minutes later there was Mark, standing there in jeans and a T-shirt that read THE MEEK WILL INHERIT THE EARTH— THE REST OF US ARE GOING TO THE STARS. He looked around Megan's space at the remnants of the mail—broken and empty shells of geometric solids, lying on the marble floor— and said, "Boy, are you ever relaxed. . . ."

Megan stood up and stretched. "Don't make me laugh," she said. "I'd be chewing my nails if I hadn't been broken of the habit long ago. This is just a handy substitute. You ready?"

Mark patted his pockets. "Armed for bear," he said. "Naturally they're going to have hefty safeguards against someone raiding their system protocols from the inside . . . but nothing equal to what I've got 'packed.' I think."

"You think?"

He shrugged. "Look, until we try, how can we be sure? We've got to seize the moment." He looked around at Megan's workspace. "Where's your friend?"

"He hasn't called yet."

Mark nodded and walked over to the edge of the "stage," looking at Saturn as it slowly rose. "I was thinking," he said, "that it might be smarter to operate this incursion out of his workspace, if he's willing. Yours has already had one interruption of the listening routines that the mole here planted in it. Whoever's behind this, if they've been watching you closely, might be suspicious about that. But Wim's space won't have been tampered with, and everything in it'll look normal to the mole."

"Right," Megan said. "He'll 'be here' in a few minutes. We can check with him then."

She reached into the air and came out with the broom that stood for her disk-cleaning program. With it Megan began sweeping up the broken shells of the discarded E-mails, and they vanished as she swept them. Mark eyed this with amusement. "Quaint," he said.

She snickered. "No more so than your feather duster." The air chimed again. She looked up. "Accept—"

There was Wim, looking unusually casual for a change, but his jeans and T-shirt and shoes were all black, a change from previous days when he had been favoring loud "resort" colors. He glanced around him, got a look at Saturn, and walked over toward that side of Megan's stage, gazing out into the darkness. "This is very impressive," he said after a few moments.

"Yeah, thanks," Megan said, and chucked her broom into the air, where it vanished. "Wim, this is Mark Gridley. He's going to help us . . . do what we have to this evening. He did your implant."

Wim came over to Mark and shook hands with him. Megan blinked. She found herself wondering whether this was the same kid she had met a few days ago, who was likely to insult you at first glance. "Megan says you're brilliant with machines," he said.

Mark nodded. "We'll find out how brilliant," he said. "I was saying to her that we ought to do this from your workspace."

"No problem," he said. "Do you need the address?"

"You have it handy?"

"Yes. The local version of it, anyway." He reached into his pocket and pulled out a glowing line of text.

Mark took it from him and studied it. "They've got both your workspaces inside a 'firewall' off to one side of the main Xanadu installation," he said.

"Is that a problem?" Wim said.

"We'll see when we get there. You want to open it up?"

Wim nodded and traced a small circle in the air at about waist height. Something appeared there: a doorknob. He took hold of it and pulled.

A door opened in the subdued lighting of Megan's workspace. Light shone through from the other side. "Come on," Wim said, and stepped through. Megan went after him, and Mark followed her.

"Jeez, Wim, what is this?" Megan said, looking up and around her as she came out on the other side, standing on cobblestones worn smooth. Blue sky shading toward the pink and orange of sunset shone above a huge three- or four-leveled courtyard with stained-glass windows. Above them, on each side, rose pointed-capped towers, each tower studded with more stained glass, pale blue-white brick shining in the sunset under the blue-tiled towers.

"It's old King Ludwig's place down in the mountains, isn't it?" Mark said, looking around. "The south of Germany."

"Neuschwanstein," Wim said, a little shyly. "We have a house near there. My father tried to buy the place once. . . ." He laughed a little, as if embarrassed. "The government wouldn't sell. But I liked it. So I borrowed it virtually, and no one seems to mind."

Megan looked around her, very impressed. People's workspaces tended to reflect the care they took about things as a rule. Some were Spartan, like Mark's, because the owner felt he or she had other more important things than interior decorating to worry about, or the person might feel that the work they did was what mattered, and they cared no more about the virtual workspace than about a regular office. But there was nothing uncaring about this. Every stone of the walls was in place; every cobblestone in the courtyard looked and felt real.

"You've done a super job here," she said. "I'd like to come back and see this someday, when we have more time."

"You are welcome," Wim said, sounding a little stiff, and a little surprised. "But what must we do now?"

Mark reached into his pocket and came up with another program symbol like the one he had given Megan to activate in her system. "Wim, can you bring up this place's directory tree?"

Wim reached up into the air and pulled it down like an old-fashioned window shade. "Thanks," Mark said, and ran the "tree" down until it showed the folder he wanted. "Here we go—"

He pushed the program in. That same high squeal ran up to the edge of hearing, but louder than Megan remembered it, and it went on for longer. Finally the pink-noise low hiss asserted itself.

Mark shook his head. "They had a lot of extra listening stuff installed in here," he said. "Does your dad use this space, too?"

"Yes. I can only use it when he isn't busy in here." Wim looked bewildered. "But he had the suite and the workspace swept for bugs when we moved in, he always does. . . ."

"Of course he would. Good standard business practice. And how many times has it been swept since?"

Wim opened his mouth, shut it again.

"Uh-huh," Mark said. "How many times have the staff been in? Changing the linens, cleaning the bathrooms, doing all those little full-service chores . . . I think a few little goodies have been left around here since you moved in. But never mind that . . . we've got other things to do." Mark turned to Megan. "You're going to have to relocate that link you found the other night."

"We can be into the virtual control area in about ten seconds," Megan said. "No need to take it slow."

"It'll certainly be alarmed," Mark said. "I plan to ignore that and head straight through, because we have other business.

"I should be able to access it with just the normal 'blanket' codes for the main Xanadu operating system. Those I've got ready. But there are likely to be addresses linked to it that your mole has trip-wired. The minute we link through one of them, he'll know that someone's on to him . . . and I'm willing to bet money that he's got security routines of his own planted around his sensitive information. We may have real trouble with those. Be ready to bail out in a hurry if you have to, and make sure the scrambler's engaged. We don't want to leave a trail."

Megan and Wim both nodded.

"Then let's do it," Mark said. "Megan?"

She nodded, looked out into the darkness. In front of her appeared the vista she and Wim had seen earlier, the virtual island of Xanadu. Megan was not going to walk across it this time, though. She dived into the darkness and flew, and the other two came fast behind her as she swooped down onto the central facility, around the back of it, and straight through the door marked STAFF ONLY, without hesitation.

It was locked against the guests of Xanadu, she knew, but it couldn't resist anyone with the access levels that the three of them shared. They shouldn't, thanks to Mark's magic touch with their implants, even trigger the alarms. In they went, and Megan stood again in the middle of that glowing webwork of light, the lines reaching out and rebounding, reaching out and rebounding, but one that did not . . .

. . . except it wasn't here.

The breath hissed out of her in fury. She spun around, looking—

"Take it easy, Megan," Mark said. "Breathe! They've just changed frequency—"

Frequency. Farther up the spectrum, or farther down—She looked around her, forcing herself to breathe, forcibly changing the way she saw the webwork. Bluer, a higher frequency—

"Nothing—" She shook her head, calmed herself, took

another big breath and forced her "vision" down lower, into the redder ranges, looking for slower datastreams, less energetic—Megan turned in a slow circle, looking around her—

Faint. Faint, but there, the one pale, dim, red thread leading out through one of the walls—

"That one!" She pointed.

Mark waded past her and seized on it.

Deeper darkness spread around them like a pool, leaving the three of them in a small circle of dimness. "I'm putting the bail-out program in," said Mark, "so we can ditch this place in a hurry if we have to. Just shout 'home' and it'll activate. We'll be dragged back to Wim's workspace immediately, with the scrambler eliminating all signs of where we've been. Ready to go?"

"Yeah," said Megan.

"Ready," Wim said.

"Step out of the light, then—"

They stepped into the darkness together. The last of the light faded behind them.

Megan caught the smell first. Food. Someone had been roasting something. There was a sweet smell as well, smoky, and a scent that reminded her of candles that had just been put out. The place was not completely dark. A faint red illumination was slowly filling everything, and there was a sound of music some ways away, horns and violins, and some very assertive singing. A shiver went along her nerves, anticipation and nervousness combined. More nervousness than she would have expected to feel.

Limbic, Megan thought, and finally it clicked—the missing connection, the thing she had been trying to remember for several days now. The limbic area didn't just process smell. It also processed fear.

She rubbed her neck thoughtfully. *Alter the implants in someone*, Megan thought, *and I'll bet you could make them feel fearful whenever you wanted. . . .*

Naturally Xanadu's guests would have their implants wiped clean of Xanadu's protocols when they left Xanadu. *But what if you were a clever technician . . . one who could make sure that bits of the coding for the implant remained in there some-*

where? So that at a crucial moment . . . you would feel an unbearable sense of terror running through you, the way I did in "Pompeii." You would feel the emotion wash over you, and be afraid . . . and not able to resist, you might—feeling the fear—do what the voice suggested. The idea had too many nasty possibilities for the kind of people in the world who really liked power. . . .

Off in the distance the singing was becoming more intense. "This is your dad's pavilion?" Mark said softly.

"Part of it," said Wim, just as quietly, sounding rather nervous. "What about the Xanadu security?"

"Outer security? We're past it."

"Just like that?"

"Not 'just,' " Mark said a little tartly. "That took me some arranging. Fortunately we have help at the top. Net Force, and my dad, came through for us. But they can't help us with the inner stuff, and we can't be sure what that's going to look like as yet. Come on."

They set out into the darkness. It grew less dark as their eyes became accustomed to it. They were moving through a huge stone-built hall, with cressets placed very high on the walls, half shielded from view by the metal brackets that held them. The light they threw from the flames burning in them was very indirect and dim. The stone floor was empty. There were a few pieces of furniture scattered around here and there—tables and chairs and couches in the old Roman style—but no sign of anything else.

"Your guy's been working on this scenario recently, I think," Mark said. "That's why the 'thread' led us straight through here."

"For all I know he is working on it now," said Wim. "We are very close to delivery time." He looked around him.

"Probably going to be a party in here pretty soon, if we wait," said Megan.

"Let's not," said Wim.

"I take it you'd rather not meet your father in the middle of all this," Mark said as they made their way toward another source of light, a doorway.

"Very much not," said Wim, sounding nervous again.

"Well," Mark said, "I have news for you. We don't have the exact location or address for the 'front door' of the pavilion, so we may have to—oops."

" 'Oops'?" Wim said as Mark flattened himself back against the wall next to the doorway. Megan flattened back, too, and hurriedly pulled Wim with her.

The music and the noise abruptly got much closer and then poured right through the doorway to their left. A crowd of very happy people in various states of dress and undress, waving cups of wine and various items of food, all came pouring through the door. In amongst them, looking unusually cheerful, was Arnulf Dorfladen, also in a toga, also equipped with a big cup of wine, being pushed and pulled along by numerous attractive females. Then came more people—musicians and jugglers and a handler with a couple of leopards on leashes. The music followed the revelers, as if someone were pushing the entire Vienna Philharmonic along behind them in a wheelbarrow. The whole entourage began to spread out, and the music got much wilder.

"It's *Tannhäuser*, all right," Megan whispered, shaking her head as she peeked around the door at the party. The pavilion builders had very accurately duplicated a racy scene from the Wagner opera in question—at least, it had been racy in 1892—the famous "Venusberg" scene, in which the goddess Venus tries to entice the disgraced knight Tannhäuser back into her magic mountain, which he had previously visited. What the magic was supposed to involve, Megan wasn't too sure, but this rendition of it seemed to involve low lighting, of the kind you might see in a really meat-rackish kind of boy-meets-girl bar, and a whole lot of amorous people dancing and eating and drinking and looking suggestively at each other. The odor of sweat and wine and incense and all the food on various suddenly overflowing banquet tables was overwhelming, and due to Xanadu's proprietary software, overwhelmingly tempting. Megan threw a cautionary look at Mark, one meant to suggest that it might not be the world's best idea to make fun of somebody's parent's fantasy, especially if that fantasy really was kind of tacky.

Wim was blinking at the passing entourage.

" 'No sex', huh?'' Megan simply had to say, but she restrained herself from any further comment.

Wim looked rueful and said nothing.

"I don't believe it," Mark said.

"What?" Megan said, in a warning tone.

"That guy over there has a hero sandwich."

Megan rolled her eyes. "Probably a programmer's joke. They have to amuse themselves somehow. Where are we going now?"

"The front door, as I was about to say. The 'indicia' will be there—the programmers' notes and remarks, and the gateway to the pavilion's basic code, if we have to go in that far."

They slipped out past the doorway, moving farther down the dimly lit hallway. "You okay?" Megan said to Wim.

His expression was a little hard to read in the dimness. "I have been worse."

They were making their way across a room now empty except for discarded wine cups on the floor and a whole lot of recently flung rose petals. At the far side of the room was a huge elaborately carved archway, with great words in some foreign script incised deeply in the arch. Mark chuckled as he saw it.

"What's so funny?" Megan said.

"Who are Nasil and Len?"

"Uh, two of the programmers."

"Well, they've signed their work. It's up there on the arch." Mark went up to the arch, ran his hands along it. "Yup," he said. "Here's the entryway to the indicia—"

He stood still, then reached into his pocket and came up with a bunch of keys, the symbols for various programming and decryption routines, and began working at the wall. Distantly Megan thought she could hear alarm bells, the kind her school would have used for fire alarms: very incongruous, in this setting. "Mark—!"

"Yeah, yeah—" He went through key after key: big iron ones, little delicate ones of the kind you might use on an old-fashioned suitcase padlock, long many-toothed ones that looked like they belonged to safe-deposit boxes—

Abruptly a patch of darkness opened in one side of the arch. "In here," Mark said, "quick!"

They slipped through. The dim red lighting behind the three of them faded away, and so did the sound of the bells. A clearer golden light fell, sourceless, from high in a new darkness that surrounded them.

Mark looked around with considerable satisfaction. "They must have been working on this pretty recently," he said.

"Yeah," Megan said. The present virtual "room" looked to be about the size of her villa's living room, and it was cluttered with solid-shape icons of all kinds, some of them stacked neatly, some of them just shoved together in heaps.

"They'll clean these out when they're sure the pavilion's running correctly," Mark said, "but these are all the source files they used to build it. All the graphics, the motion and color files, the reference files, their notes—" He glanced over them. "This place's software is a lot less proprietary than they'd like you to think," he said. "Higher bandwidth than usual, yeah, and there are some extra 'frequencies.' But the structure's overtly the same. . . ."

"What are these?" Megan said, moving over to a pile of solid icons that looked like little closed books.

Mark glanced over at them. "Some kind of scheduling files . . ."

"They're my dad's," said Wim suddenly.

"What?" Megan said.

"Look." Wim picked up one of the solids, put his thumb-nail into it and tapped it a few times. "I know the passwords for these," he said. "My dad lets me into them. They're just pages from his appointments calendar."

The solid in his hands glowed. In the air in front of him, text appeared and began to scroll. Mark came over and looked at it. "Schedule for scenario fitting," he read. "20:10 Thursday—" He tapped the "page" that hung in the air before them, and more text showed. "And a lot of other stuff. Appointments, dinners . . ."

"There are a lot more of those here," Megan said, looking at the pile of icons there, picking up another one and turning it over. "Somebody's been making copies of your dad's schedules. Business meetings, real ones and virtual—''

"My father would usually have traded partial schedule files with the people he was working with at Xanadu," Wim said. "Otherwise they would never have been able to work out when there'd be time to schedule the fittings."

"But these aren't partial files," Mark said, picking up another icon and studying it. "These are complete files. Months' worths of meetings, notes, and private information. These were encrypted . . . once."

"He got at the encryption keys somehow," Megan said, "and lifted all the files. He found out everywhere Wim's dad would be . . . and everything he would be doing, everyone he would be seeing."

" 'He,' " Wim said.

"I'll bet you money your mole is one of the two guys who was designing your dad's pavilion," Mark said. "But we don't have proof yet." Mark looked around him, then at Wim. "All of this is circumstantial at best, and it won't stand up in court. We do have at least one suggestion of how the person was able to know which virtual meeting your father was going to turn up in, and when. If he got hold of other notes of your dad's the same way, he knew exactly what to say to the people he was meeting with to produce the effects he wanted. He probably even had the minutes of the meetings that had gone before, so that if an argument started, there would be no question that he was who he was, and knew who he was talking about."

"Nasty," Megan said.

"But these are no good to me," Mark said. He chucked away the "book" icon he was holding. "I need links back to the programmer's workplace. He or she has to have a place in the Xanadu system somewhere, a space where the goodies are stored."

"A closet for the skeletons," said Wim.

Mark grinned at him. "It would be nice. If I were somebody pulling heists like this, I wouldn't keep my material in my home system. Unless I was very sure that nobody could get at it." His grin turned wolfish. "But programmers have been wrong about that before. . . .

"So let's see if this will do the trick," Mark said. He reached into his pocket and pulled out a little black box, symbol for another nest of processing routines, probably ones he preferred to keep very private. "All right," he said to it. "Scan representations in this area. Reveal common links."

Mark pointed the box at the piles of icons and slowly scanned across them. Many of them began to glow in various colors, and held the glow.

"Right," Mark muttered. He made an adjustment to his little box and turned back to the icon he had just dropped on the floor, the one for Wim's father's appointments. "Here," he said, chucking it over to Wim. "Can you find the entry for the meeting he 'didn't go to'?"

"No problem with that," Wim muttered. He touched the icon to open its coding, then twisted it in his hands until the right piece of schedule showed as text burning in the air. "Right there—"

"Thanks." Mark pointed his little black box at the text. "Read datastream and signature," he said, and then turned back toward the other piled-up icons. "Reveal common links—"

A thread of light sprang from one of the icons on the floor, shot out into the patch of darkness that had admitted them to this particular part of the pavilion space, and vanished.

"Reveal exterior link," Mark said.

The dark space in which they stood now fell away all around them, no longer seeming small and closed in. Megan could see that narrow line of light stretching away into the distance, among the many small "tent" shapes that she had seen earlier and now recognized as the Xanadu system's representation of its pavilions.

"Bingo," Mark said. "Follow the line. It leads to our mole's space, or at least to his public space in this system."

"Are you sure it's his?" Wim said.

"Why else would he have marked that particular time?" said Megan.

"But the Xanadu people were investigating," said Wim, "and they said they could find no direct linkage between their system and the virtual meeting system that our company uses—''

''Nothing direct,'' said Mark. ''I'll bet you that this linkage isn't going to be anything like direct. Besides, don't you realize how big this system is? It would take months to search it completely. Second, even if they had turned a sniffer or scanner program loose in the system-at-large, he'd have almost certainly been alerted, and he'd have moved everything. And besides—'' Mark looked smug. ''They've already searched this area, haven't they?''

''Yes.''

''Where better to hide things, then? Especially if you've been too busy to destroy them properly. Sweep them into the corner where there are already a lot of other sweepings. Detritus from a late-finished project. Hide in plain sight. Come on!''

Mark headed off along the line of the bright yellow line that reached off into the darkness. Megan and Wim hurried after him. The flat plain substituting for the ground underfoot seemed to move unnaturally quickly beneath them. Megan had an odd sense of gliding instead of running. The three of them were drawing close to the cluster of tents that were the outer representations of the pavilions—

Lightning hit the ground before them. Briefly blinded by the light, deafened by the roar, Megan couldn't see at first what had happened. She lost her balance, nearly fell, regained her balance again—and found herself staring, with the others, at Norma Wenders.

Megan drew a quick breath of panic at the sight of her, for her earlier assessment of vice-president-as-Valkyrie seemed not to have been far off. There stood Norma, spectacular in glittering full plate armor, with a sword in her hand. Megan knew that the armor was symbolic of security routines that Ms. Wenders was managing. But that did not detract from how intent and deadly she looked in that darkness, and the small angry smile on her face was very uncomfortable to see.

''I've been expecting you,'' she said.

Megan swallowed. ''We, uh—''

Ms. Wenders gestured with the sword. ''Not for very

long,'' she said. ''I came in to arrest you, originally, and it would have been such a pleasure. But I've been advised that this would presently be inadvisable. For the moment I'll go along, seeing that the request comes from unusually high levels.''

''You mean you know—?!''

She inclined her head just a little bit to Megan. ''We think something else may be about to happen this evening. Our analysis of the pattern of attacks suggests that they're getting closer together. So you three go on. I'll stand guard here; you get on with what you're doing, and don't dawdle. While you're in there, whoever's responsible for all this may bolt if they come across you. But if they do, no one will leave this space without me knowing about it . . . and believe me, if they pass here, I'll deal with them.''

Megan nodded. ''Be careful,'' she said.

''Thank you. But don't waste time. The clock's running.''

They headed past her into the darkness, at a trot.

''Friend of yours?'' said Mark as he took something else out of his pocket—apparently a small mirror. For once, he didn't sound completely self-assured.

''Oh, yeah,'' Megan said, ''absolutely. If you're nice to me, I'll introduce you.''

''You do that,'' Mark said. He sounded just a little strangled.

Megan smiled just slightly.

They followed the line of light through the virtual landscape, past various of the tents. It seemed to arrow into one of them a good distance away but did not stop there—merely continued on through it and out the other side. They ran straight along the line, but just shy of the tent Mark, with his mirror held out, stopped, and Megan and Wim stopped with him.

''What? What?'' Wim said.

''Half a second,'' Mark said, and pulled something else out of his pocket. Megan blinked. It was an old-fashioned ear trumpet, such as deaf people had used two centuries back. He laid it carefully against the tent, then listened through it with exaggerated care.

A subdued bleat of noise came through it, but not so subdued that Mark didn't flinch back. "Ow!"

"What?" Megan said.

Mark shook his head. "You wouldn't have liked that in your central nervous system," he said. "Which is where it would have wound up. Our little friend left it for us. Now, then—" He pulled out the neck of the trumpet, and out, and out, until it stretched clear around and Mark bent it back toward the tent—

Megan heard a vague odd squawking sound, after which silence fell again. Mark chuckled. "I don't think he'll try that one again any time soon," he said. "Feedback. If he was listening then, I feel sorry for him. Let's get back on the line—"

They got back on it, slipping through the "tent"—

—through what seemed the middle of a play. All around them was a large circular wooden theater space, and the area around the stage was crowded with people in what looked like Elizabethan-era clothing. They were shouting and laughing at something that was happening, but all of them stopped to stare at three strangely-dressed children appearing out of nowhere, running through the place, and out the other side again. Shouts of astonishment broke out and were lost again into the silence of the darkness outside the tents—

"That was interesting," Wim said.

"Must ask about that one later," Megan said.

"Hurry up!" Mark said.

They ran. Another tent loomed in front of them. "Keep going!" Mark said, holding the mirror out in front of him and checking it. "We're clear, no traps—"

They ran through the tent—

—and ran full tilt into a wall.

"Aha," Mark said, when he managed to pick himself up again. "So finally he begins to show some sense."

"Ow. Not a trap then," Megan said, picking herself up. "But a dead end, for which you forgot to check."

"Not quite. Password lock." Mark was fumbling around in his pocket again. "Now, where did I put—aha."

He came up with something else, not a black box or a

mirror this time, but a small convoluted dingus that seemed to be made of glass.

"What are you doing?" Wim said.

Mark slapped the little glass contraption up against the all-too-solid wall of the tent. "This is a password cracker," he said. "It contains, courtesy of Xanadu, the complete personnel files of everyone who works for the place. Every nickname, address, commlink number, and other piece of trivia associated with every one of them. With any luck, he'll have used something familiar, and this'll be fast. If not, the cracker starts testing different languages, then it works its way through every conceivable random combination of letters and numbers. If it resorts to that, we'll be here awhile."

"We can hope we'll be spared," Megan breathed.

The cracker flickered gently to itself. Mark smiled. "Bets?" he said. "Lay them now while you can."

Megan just shook her head.

The cracker flashed white.

"That's it," he said. He glanced at the cracker. "The Latin name for his birthstone," he said. "I don't believe it. But that's the problem with programmers. They get clumsy."

"You're a programmer," Wim said.

Mark made a small feral grin. "Not a clumsy one. Now, then . . ."

He reached up to pull the cracker off the tent wall. "Once I remove this," he said, "we have to move really fast. Odds are that he's somewhere in the system, live, and when we break in here, if we haven't found all the traps and avoided them, alarms will go off. He could be on us in minutes. I've got some nasty blocks preprogrammed to throw in his way— but he's really good and he'll probably be able to circumvent them soon enough if we catch his attention. Ready?"

"Yeah," Megan said, and Wim nodded.

"Come on—"

They stepped through the wall of the tent.

It was like a vast warehouse filled with junk: half-built structures, piles of icons both tidy and messy, piles of virtual paper that were symbols for text files, small nondescript cog-and-gear machines that represented programs of various kinds. "What a mess," Mark said. "I bet this guy takes his laundry home to his mother, too."

They moved hurriedly among the icons and the bric-a-brac, the shelves and half-built, half-drawn trees and archways and empty door frames.

"Aha," Mark said again, for off to one side, sitting on a tripod, was a satellite dish.

They gathered hurriedly around it. "A little small, isn't it?" Wim said.

"It's a symbol," Mark said, and took hold of it, lifted it down. "Yesss—"

The air all around them came alive with diagrams and times and dates of satellite feed connections, angles and positions on the Clarke Belt above the curve of an unseen Earth. "Yes, indeed," Mark said. "Very complicated, some of these. Too circuitous. Why would anyone bother with comms routings like these if they didn't have something to hide? Our boy—I think we can assume it's one of the two—has put this one call through three different comm satellites . . . and there can be only one reason for that kind of thing. Hiding your trail . . . But look where it went."

He pointed, tracing a route from Xanadu to a geosynch satellite over the Caribbean, to another over West Africa, to another in the Far East, to a ground station, and then up again to another satellite serving Europe. "Bounce, bounce, bounce . . ." Mark said. "Look there. Look at the timing. That's your London one, Megan—the poor guy who vanished later. And Wim, look, here's the link that led us here. Your dad's 'meeting.' " Mark looked around him in excitement. "This is it. This is pay dirt—"

Megan turned away and looked out into the dimness that surrounded them. Off to one side was something that looked entirely more finished than anything else here, a sleek shape, dark, big. "Mark," she said.

"Megan, we've got enough, we should get out and tell the people who run this place before—"

"No," Megan said, and hurried over toward that sleek object. Short, almost stubby cylindrical body, three long swap-in-swap-out ion/chemical boosters, the big wide cockpit window, almost a trademark of the design since it had first been launched—

"What the heck is this?" Mark said.

"It's the space jeep," said Wim.

"But not the usual one," Megan said. "Mark, look at it. Look at the booster packs. They're not the usual ones. They're bigger."

"I don't get it," Mark said.

Megan ran a hand along the shining hull. "This is something new. A new prototype . . ."

"Whatever, it looks like someone has plans for it," Mark said, wandering over to a stack of papers, an icon for something else hidden in the system.

He pointed at the stack of papers, snapped his fingers. It was an icon, as Megan had expected, and suddenly the air around them was filled with scrolling text, and here and there a few windows with images in them. Most of them were of people sitting in implant lineup chairs or before solid-image cameras, caught still in mid-word.

"Someone's been in High Black's records," Wim said. "The way they got into my dad's."

"And they pulled this stuff out," Mark said. "Probably the same way, while they were in supposedly helping Rigel with his schedule for his 'fittings.' The whole hardware package. All the development information . . . all here."

Megan turned hurriedly away, picking up another "pile of paper," which promptly turned into more scrolling text. "Boeing, fifty billion . . . AST, sixty-five billion . . ." She looked up in astonishment. "These are bids," she said. "Someone wants this prototype. Not the people who it's supposed to go to, either. Not the little companies, the little countries." She scanned hurriedly down the text. "Here are some more—they just want to cannibalize the hardware for other projects—" She swallowed, horrified.

Wim picked up another of the "piles of paper"—then nearly dropped it. "This has numbers on it," he said.

"What?"

Mark came over and took it from him, shook the icon. Along with much other text, it abruptly unfolded a stopwatch-patch into the air, a digital readout frozen in tenths and hundredths of a second, with about half an hour left to run. "What's going to happen when this goes off?" she said.

"Let's see if we can find out," said Mark. He reached down into the text, tapped at several lines of it, then started pulling it out of the air in a long ribbon.

"What? What are you talking about?" Megan cried.

"You don't get it, Megan," said Mark, sounding angry. "All of this is just circumstantial evidence. Electron trail, yes. But it's not enough . . . it won't stand up in a court of law. And what's the point if that's not where this ends?" He kept pulling the text out. "This has to stop. All of this. And what has to happen, is that the perp himself has to put in an appearance and link himself with the evidence. Otherwise nothing stands up—"

He said nothing more for several moments. Megan and Wim looked over their shoulders.

Mark sighed and let the long ribbon of text snap back into place in the "pile of paper."

The stopwatch, reset to fifteen minutes, began counting down.

"We've got a few seconds yet," Mark said. "Not too long, though. He'll know the time is wrong. He has to react. And he'd better. Because as for this—" He gulped. "It looks like they're going to go into Rigel's computers and crash everything," he said. "Not to mention the computers themselves. This routine will fry them physically. And then a second time cycle begins. A couple of days, while the other companies sort out the bids . . . or don't. Some of the variables are still empty, or they have conditionals hooked to them. If no one bids high enough—" He pulled and pulled at the data, and abruptly came up with a tangled mass of light, a great complicated knot of logic and programming inextricably interwoven with itself. He hissed a frustrated breath out through his teeth. "They're going to destroy the whole space jeep project," Mark said. "Just destroy it. And the ability to re-create it. All gone."

And Rigel's dream comes crashing down, Megan thought. *He loses. Everyone loses.*

"We've got to stop it," she said.

"This guy's a nasty type," said Mark. "But we shouldn't have to wait long before he puts in an appearance. There's one more thing I want to check—"

He went off to one side, past what at first appeared to be clothing racks, the kind you would hang out-of-season clothes on in the garage. Wim stopped and stared at these. "Look at all this stuff," he breathed.

Megan paused by him, her heart beating fast. There were masks, racked up. Empty human skins—or so they seemed— hung up on hangers, like clothes waiting to be put on. Folded suits piled up on the floor.

"Identities, waiting to be assumed," Mark said softly, moving among them while he sought something else. The hanging figures were male and female, old and young, people of every kind and nationality. "This guy's been acquiring lives."

"And look at this," said Megan. She walked over to a dark window that hung in the air, peered through it. Visible on the far side was a blueprint-style diagram of what appeared to be a Renaissance mansion. Bright lines indicated what looked to Megan like access routes. Here and there codes were indicated, electrical or numerical "keys" that would open doors or gates.

"It's the Miami robbery," Megan said. "The guy James Winters told me about."

"He's keeping souvenirs of his crimes," Wim said. "Serial killers do that, don't they?"

"Yeah." Mark looked disgusted. "What we've got here is more like a serial robber. But I bet the motivation's pretty much the same. While he's planning other robberies, he can go back and relive these whenever he likes. And—"

He reached out to one very tall "pile of paper" not far away. The top unfolded another stopwatch, this one frozen with no display, but ready to go. "Just as I thought," Mark said, sounding seriously alarmed now. "That small 'other problem.' Logic bomb—"

Wim whirled. "Bomb? Where?"

"Not that kind," Mark said. "A set of programming instructions left in the system. Usually for malicious purposes. So that if, say, a programmer gets fired—all kinds of data in the system can be corrupted. Even destroyed. The whole system could wipe itself out. And other events can be triggered elsewhere, just before it goes—''

Megan swallowed hard at the thought. The malice that their ''mole'' had shown so far was unrelenting. Who knew what he might be thinking of doing, how many innocents he would hurt—

''Mark, never mind that now. There's more important business. Get back there, and whatever you do, undo that knot!''

He started back that way. ''I may have to cut it.''

''I don't care if you have to eat it. Just don't let those prototypes get destroyed!''

—and suddenly someone came in through the wall of the space and stared at them in shock.

Len MacIlwain, that gentle geeky look of his twisting through rage, out into shock.

''GOTCHA!'' Mark cried in triumph. Len ran straight out again, into the darkness: gone.

And atop that particularly tall stack of paper, the ''stopwatch'' popped into existence and began to run down with frightful speed.

''Get him!'' Wim yelled. ''He's the one!''

''I'll get him,'' Megan said. ''Wim, come with me. Mark—!''

''Don't wait for me!'' Mark shouted at her. ''Go, I'll be right behind you! Find him! Don't lose him, he'll try to go to ground somewhere!''

''But he'll double back—''

''I've blocked off the network path behind us! Run, Megan, just find him, run, and don't let him out of your sight!''

Megan ran, out of the part-built pavilion, out into the darkness. In the virtual world your mind conquered, and Megan's mind knew that she was fit, perfectly able to chase MacIlwain down like a deer. She ran. He ran. What Wim was doing behind her, she didn't care. Her whole attention was on MacIlwain in front of her, running, but not as fast as she was. He ran at a pavilion, into it, through it. Megan ran after him.

Flick, and they were in some kind of desert, something huge
was rumbling under the sand. He ran in front of her, out into
nothingness, and Megan ran straight after him, and out the
other side. Darkness again, and MacIlwain in front of her,
and the tent-walls of another pavilion in front. Flick, straight
through it, and there was nothing but starry night sky all
around it, and MacIlwain running through it ahead of her, and
Megan right behind. Flick, out the other side again, and into
the darkness between the tents. Someone was just behind her.
Wim. Good for him—

A stitch was starting in Megan's side, and she ignored it.
Another tent loomed before her. Flick, straight into it. Some
rain-foresty setting, some sort of primates howling hysteri-
cally in the trees, MacIlwain pounding through the leaf mold
ahead of her, Megan right behind. Flick, out the other side.
The stitch was getting worse, but it was just virtual pain, and
even if it had been real, it wouldn't have stopped her. She'd
dealt with these enough in real life. Run through it, run out
the other side of the pain, run into your second wind . . .

Ahead of her MacIlwain was slowing down. Flick, and
there was the Shakespeare play again. They plunged through
it, the crowd roaring behind them, out the other side. A
thrown orange flew past her nose as she ran through. Another
one missed Wim, who was still with her, just behind. *Amazing, didn't think he had it in him.* Flick, another jungle, this
one on some alien planet under a triple moon, out the other
side. Flick, the hot blue of Jacob Rigel's reef. Flick, through
the *Tannhäuser* bacchanalia again, a storm of food and singing. Flick, flick, flick, through maybe ten or fifteen other pavilions that Megan barely noticed, she was so intent on the
back of the fleeing man in front of her, and so angry. *He has
back doors into every pavilion here. How long has he been
studying the clients, one after another, using the personal
information that they trustingly gave the programmers working for them, hunting weaknesses in their lives, ways to get
at their wealth and power, to target them, to punish them for
their success—*

But flick, and suddenly it changed, and Megan knew something different was going to happen. This pavilion had

nothing inside it but bare tent walls. Partial programming structures, half wire frame, half completed textured solids, stood around in it. Not completely engineered. MacIlwain ran at the far wall—

—bounced off it.

He scrambled to his feet, gasping, and turned at bay. There was nowhere left to go.

"Don't make me hurt you," he said as Megan thumped to a stop in front of him, as Wim came up behind and nearly slammed into her back. The programmer's words were almost a snarl.

"Oh, like you haven't hurt other people?" Megan shouted. "Like you weren't going to hurt all the people Jacob Rigel is going to be able to help? Don't make me laugh."

"I won't, then," Len MacIlwain said—

—and the fear hit Megan like a sledgehammer, and smashed her down.

She gasped, tried to get her breath, but couldn't. She felt like something huge and terrible was staring down at her, about to do something horrible to her, anything it wanted.

Off to one side she could see Wim collapse to his knees as well. "Don't," he moaned, "don't, please—"

Megan gasped and tried to push herself up, but her limbs wouldn't obey her. Suddenly a third set of footsteps echoed in the space. "Megan!" Mark's voice cried. "What is it?"

Megan could barely speak, the fear compressed her chest so. *It's like a heart attack,* she thought. *I'm dying. . . .* But at the same time something in the back of her head said, furious, *It's not. It's the implant! He's using it—*

"Limbic" was all she could get out. There was no breath to speak with.

She just managed to turn her head enough to see Mark stare, astonished, and then collapse, too.

Oh, no. No.

Megan could just see MacIlwain come stalking over to them, that gentle, geekish look on his face gone entirely nasty. He glanced at Mark, then away again, and strolled over to her. "Poor Megan," he said. "You weren't in enough trouble when La Wenders caught you the other day, were you? Nothing like you're in now. They're going to have a lot of trouble figuring out why you suddenly just had a heart attack. Someone as young and fit as you, too. Or why you should suddenly have a stroke," he said, stepping over to Wim and giving him a nasty kick in the side. Helpless, Wim rolled and moaned on the blackness of the floor. "Well, it happens when you bypass the usual screenings we give people before accepting them for pavilion access."

He turned away toward Mark. Megan had been waiting for that. Slowly she pushed herself up on her elbows. *I will not— will not—it's not me. I'm not afraid. It's the implant—*

"As for your buddy here," Len said, "doubtless he's some good last-minute idea of La Wenders's. Too bad for him, his parents are going to be so upset when he—"

The next sound out of his lips was a strangled *Ggk!*—and Len MacIlwain's face contorted in surprise as he reacted in the only possible way to being kicked in the solar plexus by Megan O'Malley. He folded in half and fell down.

"No, they won't," Megan said, still panting with fear, and the effort of beating it, as she stood there over him, slightly hunched over, and ready to kick him again.

"Fortunately," she said, "I've had this—tried on me before. And I—beat it last time. And this time—I knew what to do about it. Reset—to default. Pain settings where they belong—at normal. And fear—"

She wiped away the sweat that was running into her eyes, and started pushing herself back up to her feet. "Come on, you guys," she said. "Get up. It's just scared. And not even real scared. Fake scared. Your implants are resetting right now. Get up, shake it!"

They were shaking it already. Mark was standing up, and Wim was on his hands and knees. Mark was actually acquiring a rather feral grin as his implant reset, as Megan had suggested it do. "And you, you poor idiot," Mark said, "are history. You and your logic bomb together . . . because I took it apart. Jacob Rigel's prototypes for the space jeep will go just where they're scheduled to go. You and your nasty little plans, however, are going into some secure facility as an example of how not to commit virtual crime. Now that you have so kindly presented us with the perpetrator, in the flesh . . . as it were.''

MacIlwain writhed on the floor, clutching his gut, and began to scream, a horrible strangled sound. ''I hate them!'' he screamed. ''Why should they have so much when so few of us have anything at all? Why can't we take what they have if we're smart enough? It's not fair! Why can't we be rich? Why can't we be famous? Why can't we be happy?''

Megan went over to help Wim up, but he didn't need that much help, though they staggered against each other as she tried to help him.

''He doesn't sound too good,'' Wim said.

''Good. He deserves not to,'' Megan said.

Mark was looking down at MacIlwain with some amusement.

''As for the last few questions,'' Mark said conversationally, ''I can't help you. But I can tell you that you're never going to get anywhere if you use a birthday as a password. Even your mother's birthstone, or her birthday. Do you know how short the algorithm is for finding a password based on a—''

MacIlwain screamed again, lost in mindless fury.

''Let's get out of here,'' Mark said. ''This guy's got no conversation. Back the way we came, in one long hop. Got the address? One, two, three—''

''Megan?'' her father was shouting. ''Megan! Megan!''

The door. *Oh God, I locked it.* Megan staggered woozily to the door, and let her father in, moaning. All her muscles were cramping—adrenaline overload, probably. Nothing like that had ever happened to her before after a VR session, but then she'd never experienced VR quite this way before, either. Her head felt like someone had been hitting it with hammers.

''Megan, honey, are you all right?'' her father said urgently, catching her. ''Megan!''

''I'm okay,'' she said. ''I'm okay. I was scared, but it's all over.'' She leaned on him, hid her face on his shoulder. ''Oh, boy,'' she said, ''was I scared.''

But at the same time, she was proud of herself. *I beat it*, she thought. *I knew it wasn't me.* "We won," she said.

"You got your man?"

"We got him." She took a long deep breath and stood up straight. "One thing, though, Dad."

"What, honey? Anything you like."

"I don't ever want to go to see *Tannhäuser* again," she said.

She patted him on the back and staggered off down the hall into her bedroom. "Again?" her father said behind her, bemused. "We've never been before."

Megan laughed, fell face forward on her bed, and passed out.

She slept very late the next day. That afternoon was a good one for her, though. When Megan headed down to the kitchen, the first voice she heard was her mother's, saying, "Sweetheart, where did these lobsters come from?" And the next sound she heard was the blessed noise of her brothers, all of them, rejoicing in the sight of a full refrigerator. She could only imagine their glee when they discovered it was apparently refilled every fifteen minutes.

"So much for peace and quiet," she said. But in the aftermath of the previous night, Halvarson had insisted that the whole family come down to Xanadu. Now there were adolescent and postadolescent males trampling all over the place, shouting about windsurfing and snorkeling and who knew what else.

"It was so nice there for a while," Megan said, with just the slightest annoyance, to her father later that day.

"I know," her father said. "All I can say is, you've brought it on yourself. Too much success . . ."

Megan shook her head. "Gratitude," she said, "can go too far." Then she laughed. "Never mind . . . I'll take it up with him later."

She headed out to the beach later that morning, intending to take time to really enjoy it for the first time, rather than using it as an anti-listening device. To her considerable surprise she found not only Wim out there, sitting calmly and staring out at the water, but also his father, lying on his back on a foam beach mattress and turning an unbecoming shade of pink.

She went up to him, gazed down on him, and said, "Hi." She might have been nonplussed by him before, but now Megan had seen Dorfladen Senior in a toga, flushed with wine and fantasy, and was much less impressed by anything he might do or say.

He looked up at her with those cold little eyes and said, "Young lady, I have much to thank you for, they tell me."

"Thank Wim," Megan said. "If it wasn't for him, I wouldn't have bothered."

Dorfladen's eyebrows went up at that. "You will doubtless have a terrible management style some day," he said. "Then I thank you, my son."

Wim looked at his father with complete astonishment. "You're welcome."

Arnulf Dorfladen grunted and turned over on his stomach.

It is something cultural, Megan thought, *but don't ask me what*. To Wim she said, "How much longer will you be here?"

"A few days." They took a few steps away from Dorfladen Senior. "We have to file criminal charges with the international authorities who will be prosecuting MacIlwain . . . then get back to putting my father's companies back together."

"You'd think," Megan said softly, "that he might thank you a little more emphatically. Considering what you've done."

"Considering that he's never thanked me in front of anyone else before, not in my entire life," Wim said, just as softly, "I don't feel so bad."

She gave him a long look . . . then nodded.

"When do you leave?" Wim said.

"We have another week. Recovery time," Megan said.

Wim nodded. "When you get home," he said, "give me a call. I will show you the Mad King's castle."

"I'll do that," Megan said.

Wim nodded. "And thanks," he said, "for knocking me over."

Then he turned and walked away, back to his father.

Megan smiled, and walked away, too.

It was that evening at the usual soirée in the main facility, while her mother and father were dancing and her brothers were attempting to demolish the buffet, that Halvarson took Megan aside to thank her privately. "Of course," he said, "we're not going to be able to publicize what you've done here. It would be unwise."

"I would agree," she said.

"But you're welcome to come back," Halvarson said, "whenever your father's schedule makes it possible. That would need to be your cover, of course. Otherwise it would look . . . a little strange."

"Of course," she said.

"Naturally we're going to look into our personnel screening," said Halvarson. "And we're looking at the possibility of adjusting our implants. It will no longer be possible to use them to scare a person to death."

"I'm glad to hear that," Megan said, rubbing her neck.

He nodded to her, patted her shoulder, and moved on to greet some new guest.

Megan sat there and reached out for the glass of champagne he had brought her. Out on the dance floor her mother and father were smiling at each other. Her brothers were flirting with some of the other guests. Her oldest brother was smiling at Norma Wenders in a way that suggested he considered her the best-looking thing in the place. Megan glanced at Ms. Wenders, who glanced back at her, if coolly, and very slightly lifted her own glass.

Megan smiled and had a sip of her own champagne.

It's nice to be rich, she thought, *at least temporarily.* And she headed over to the buffet to get at the lobster before her brothers could finish it off.

The next morning she finally caught up with James Winters for her debrief. Mark had already filled him in on his own side of things, and most of the data they needed to understand what Len MacIlwain had been up to was now in place, though some of it would take weeks more to tease out of the many places in Xanadu where he had hidden it.

"He had apparently been at this for a long time, in a small way," Winters said. "His family was never terribly well off, and originally he started by stealing credit. It's a big business. A lot of people do it, though most of them aren't expert, and they get caught. Your boy Len became expert, though. He started small—mining extinct birth and death records and such for identities of people who once existed legally but didn't anymore. Then he got bolder. He started stealing the identities of people who did exist."

Winters sat back in his chair. "That's a more dangerous game. It's not rare, either, but people tend to get caught at it faster. The world is just too interconnected these days. You're too likely to run into someone who 'saw' you somewhere where they knew you weren't going to be. Again, though, Len was clever. He watched his targets carefully, studied them thoroughly so that he knew their moves, their friends, the places on-line or off-line where they hung out. He started pilfering other people's accounts and belongings. He was as good at the physical kind of pilfering as the virtual kind, and he had some skill with disguise as well. If he thought the authorities were getting too close to him, he made himself a new identity and moved on. He got really good at it."

"Good enough to get Xanadu to hire him," Megan said.

"That's right. They did their usual background checks, but they couldn't find anything that seemed out of place. Of course he had forged most of his references, and some of the identities of the people in them, so when the Xanadu staff people followed some of the references up, it was Len they wound up talking to . . . though they didn't know it. Other references were real. He fooled them."

"And then," Megan said, "he was in paradise. Sitting in the middle of one of the most powerful and exclusive private computer networks in the world . . . with free access to everything. And lots of information about its clients."

Winters nodded. "He got greedy," he said. "That was his downfall. Dorfladen was the key, the one case in which MacIlwain got not only greedy but also careless. He had been so successful that he didn't think he'd have to worry about anything anymore. His programming had already been closely audited by Norma Wenders and her own private security team, previously, and he didn't think he had anything to fear from them, not while he kept moving his password clusters around. Then he made his hit and removed the obvious traces so that the audit wouldn't show anything. But you found the right spot to look . . . the already-audited records. He wasn't counting on someone checking the barn, so to speak, after the horses had already been stolen and the barn had been closed. . . ."

Megan nodded. "That was Mark's call."

"All the same, you put him on the track. You did a good job, Megan. Don't belittle your part in it."

"All right," she said. "One thing, though."

"I am entirely at your disposal."

"I thought you were going to be deploying Net Force personnel down there."

"I did," Winters said.

Megan made an amused face at him. "I mean, adult Net Force personnel."

"I did," Winters said.

"Who?" Megan said.

Winters smiled at her. "I'm going to leave that as an exercise for the student," he said. "But not all our personnel are overt. Some of them prefer to work quietly in places where they can feed their caffeine habits. Meanwhile . . . I think you should get back to your vacation. School starts all too soon . . . and there is no hope for potential future operatives who don't keep their grades up."

She sighed. "Mr. Winters . . . you're worse than my father."

"I accept that as the compliment you no doubt intended it to be," said James Winters. "Now get out of here and go finish your vacation. I wish I could have one of those, by the way."

Megan waved goodbye to him and let Winters's office vanish, then stood up and went off to go see a man about a trilobite.